DISTANT LEGACY

CONSCRIPTION DAY

BY NIGEL SCHAEFER

 FriesenPress

Suite 300 - 990 Fort St
Victoria, BC, V8V 3K2
Canada

www.friesenpress.com

Editor: Brian Baxter

ISBN
978-1-03-911887-4 (Hardcover)
978-1-03-911886-7 (Paperback)
978-1-03-911888-1 (eBook)

1. FICTION, DYSTOPIAN

Distributed to the trade by The Ingram Book Company

This book is dedicated to the men and women who influenced me and made me the man I am today.

PROLOGUE

WAR. WE ALL KNOW what "war" means. It's fairly easy just to research "war" on the internet, which will yield something along the lines of: "A state of armed conflict between two states or nations or groups within a nation or state."

All of us understand what war means, but half the time we don't know why the state of armed conflict ever begins. While the reason for the war this story is about has been lost, this world war has been an active conflict for the past thirty or so years, which is almost as old as I am.

We don't remember if the communists want complete domination or if they got off on the wrong foot with Uncle Sam. They might have economic or national reasons, or maybe there is a communist Hitler on the block that we haven't heard of. Religion could be the unlikely catalyst, because every country in the Eastern Powers of Communism (EPC) believes in a different religion.

I'm honestly surprised the communists haven't started an ideological war with themselves!

So, no one really remembers how or why this war started, and no one knows how it's going to end.

My name is Gary Foltz, and this is my story.

"Good morning, Mr. Foltz, My name is Dr. Brooks. I am your designated psychologist. Before we start, tell me about yourself before you were conscripted into the Canadian Armed Forces."

"Why am I here? Please tell me," I said nervously. "I think I am fine in my current mental state."

"Well," Dr. Brooks continued, "According to your body language and tone, and that you haven't had a proper shower in twelve years, I would say you aren't ok and you are clearly not mentally stable."

"To make this process easier, let us start from the beginning, like, where were you born, what was your home life like before you went to university, and what your life was like before you went to boot camp."

"Well, my life was fairly simple. I grew up just outside of the city of Winnipeg in the province of Manitoba in Canada. I was born on June 8, 2026. My father, Patrick Foltz, was an engineer. My mother, Eleanor Foltz, was a nurse. I have an older brother, Ethan, who drove tanks in Europe and Africa. I learned how to ride a bike when I was five years old."

"I walked through school with no problems. After high school I entered the University of Alberta with multiple scholarships and earned my master's degree in Math and Weaponized Robotics free of charge."

"I taught Math and Science as a substitute teacher for about two years before I was conscripted into the Canadian Armed Forces. As a CAF conscriptee, I was sent to British Columbia to fight the EPC. There you go. That was my life. Can I leave now?!?" I asked impatiently.

"Sorry, Mr. Foltz, I don't think I can let you do that. Let's start simple. Tell me about boot camp."

┌ CHAPTER 1 ┐
The War with Yourself

STARTED MY STORY. "WHEN we entered our training facility on the first day of boot camp, we started training immediately. As soon as our training started, I regretted my decision to obey our prime minister!"

"I could have fled to Mexico or South Africa, but I knew that no matter where I could have fled to, there was a conflict of some kind. During that time Mexico was sending their army to Australia or Europe by way of America, and South Africa was the main supplier of help aid in the upcoming African campaign."

"Sorry," Dr. Brooks interrupted, "your file says that you were conscripted in 2051, but Africa was invaded four years later, in '56."

I clarified by saying, "We knew they were coming."

Dr. Brooks encouraged explanation by asking, "How did you know they were coming?"

I continued. "Africa was one of the main supply lines to Europe for oil, natural metals, food, and foreign supplies from South America, Canada and the United States. The EPC generals would be idiots if they didn't consider taking North Africa to swing the odds in their favour."

My answer apparently impressed Dr. Brooks, and he pressed for more detail. "So, instead of avoiding the inevitable, you ran in head first! Is that correct?"

When I heard that, I back-pedalled a little. "Well, when you say it like that, you make me sound like I am an idiot." I was not too pleased with Dr. Brooks' insinuation!

Trying to smooth an awkward blunder, Dr. Brooks also back-pedalled. "Saying that you wanted to avoid the inevitable was more of a compliment to you, because you did not want to be an idiot by breaking the law, but…" Dr. Brooks pulled himself emotionally out of the conversation and continued as an impartial interviewer. "You can interpret our conversation however you want." Then, to get back to the information he really wanted, Dr. Brooks continued, "Now, Gary, let's get back to your description of boot camp."

I continued. "Well, basic training, or 'boot camp,' as you like to call it, usually takes about ten weeks. In addition to basic training, we all needed infantry training. And that alone was a joke, to say the least!"

My comment on infantry training surprised Dr. Brooks. "How was infantry training a joke?"

I explained, "The training normally takes about seventeen weeks, so to be 'fit for battle' my teammates and I needed twenty-seven weeks of training." Then I smirked and maliciously continued, "We got three whole days of infantry training! After those ever-so-precious three days we were deployed two days after our training!"

Dr. Brooks wanted to focus on the infantry training. "So explain to me those three days of infantry training."

I obliged. "On day one, we were all assigned to different teams and assigned roles within those teams. Each of us was also trained for our assigned role. I was assigned to be a point man. My role as point man meant that I was always at the front of the team beside the commanding officer of my unit."

"Day two was a briefing in a lecture hall. The lecture hall could sit hundreds of people. They handed out handbooks two hundred pages thick. The handbook details the theory of every possible danger on the battlefield. On the third day they gave us the whole day just to read the book."

"Remember when I said the handbook detailed the theory of every possible battlefield danger? Well, no matter how hard our trainers tried to impress us from theory, they could not prepare us for the reality of infantry combat!"

"Sure, each of our uniforms showed that we were 'fit for battle,' but none of us had had any experience in war. Our superiors did their best with the tools they had available, I don't doubt that for a moment. Unfortunately, the only damn thing I remember from that ridiculous book is what an EPC uniform looks like. Everything else that I learned about survival on the battlefield, I learned in Princeton."

I continued, "When my unit got deployed into British Columbia in September 2051, we didn't even get to go to our bunks! As soon as we got off the helicopter transports, we were rushed to our briefing and then to our unit assignments. Immediately after our briefing and receiving our unit assignments, we were sent to the front line. Chief Warrant Officer Andrews commanded my unit."

Andrews had wasted no time in barking at us, "Alright, gentlemen, we suspect the EPC will attack the town of Princeton for the fourth time this week. The Royal 22nd Regiment has successfully defended Princeton against the EPC's three earlier attacks. We have the honour of relieving the regiment of their position!"

"Any questions?" Andrews asked.

I was thinking, "Any questions? We had hardly had time to really understand what was being asked of us and we were being asked if we had questions? On the other hand, the entire situation was specifically designed to overwhelm us and put our brains into survival mode – quite effective!"

"Good!" Andrews continued. Andrews knew that we had not had time to formulate questions because he had done his job of putting our brains into survival mode.

Andrews continued to overwhelm us with more information. "Lieutenant Umbach will show us the defensive positions, medical tents, and ammo storage when we arrive."

I volunteered some information to Dr. Brooks about Andrews out of respect for Andrews. "Andrews is a good leader. Andrews had seen his fair share of battles. He fought in Europe, as a rookie in 2039, when he was eighteen, until he was twenty-four. He lost an arm and half of a leg during his time on the European front in the Ukraine. After all the rehab and medical procedures, Andrews came back to Europe five years later, in 2050 with cybernetic enhancements and a hunger to beat the enemy. Andrews was still very unlucky. Six months later he came back to Europe with chemical burns on his neck, face, and upper body. Anyways, after four months of healing from the burns, Andrews was awarded a Victorian Cross and got to command his own unit, which is the unit that I was assigned to twelve years ago in Princeton."

"Please explain what fighting in Princeton was like for you," said Dr. Brooks.

"It was the first time in my life I had seen combat. The things I saw and did there changed me forever. It was physically and mentally difficult," I replied.

Dr. Brooks probed further. "Please explain what was difficult about your time there."

I continued, "Well, there were twelve hundred men deployed with my unit on September 4, 2051, to Princeton, BC."

Dr. Brooks confirmed, "You said there were twelve hundred of you when you got there?"

I verified, "Yes."

Dr. Brooks wanted to get an idea of how dangerous our mission was. "Of the original twelve hundred, how many of you survived?"

Remembering the answer was mentally difficult. "Five!" I stammered to continue, "just five of us survived. There was Andrews, Fernsby, Weppler, a medic named Colson, and myself."

Dr. Brooks wanted to draw the story out of me. "How did you survive there for so long?"

I resisted saying, "It's a long story that I would rather not get into." I knew Dr. Brooks expected my response. I also knew

I really did not feel like going there at the moment. Dr. Brooks and I were at a stalemate as to how he would get me past this place of mental protectiveness.

He pressed softly. "The only way I can help you, Gary, is if you tell me what happened."

I had expected Dr. Brooks to press softly, and I knew it was his job to do so. I did feel he was genuine in his attempt to help me, so I carefully asked for reassurance. "You promise that this will help me?"

Dr. Brooks refocussed my attention. "Only if you tell me what happened in Princeton."

"Ok," I reluctantly continued. "When we got off the trucks in Princeton, we didn't know what we were getting into. Our orders were simply to 'Hold the line!'"

"On the first day we were all shown around. We were shown where everything was. We were shown everything from the bathroom to the machine-gun nest. We were even shown that my squad was stationed on the southwest side of town. Elsewhere in Princeton, there was an inn across from a gas station. North of the inn was a church of some kind. West of the inn was a school, and north of the school was a lodge and a hospital."

I continued, "Each of those buildings had a role to play in our defense; the inn had a hole in the roof, so it was a great spot for a mortar pit. The gas station had no gasoline but the building had been reinforced and outfitted with heavy weapons and ammo. The gas station was our first line of defense on the western front. The church was the middleman for all the supplies. If we needed supplies at the gas station, they would take them through the church. The school was where we slept, and where all our supplies of food, ammo, and medicine were stored. Every time someone was delivering supplies, you had to pick the supplies up from the school, go to the church to get inspected and be given your route to your drop off, and then navigate the route. The hospital was the first-aid station for the wounded, and where we received supplies on a weekly basis. The weekly supplies got sent to the school until we were cut off after a week of fighting."

A concerned Dr. Brooks asked, "How did you and the men handle being cut off from your weekly supply drop?"

I explained, "Well, our superiors told us that we were not in a position to fix the problem, so we had to start rationing supplies. The rationing made our supplies last about a month."

A clearly impressed Dr. Brooks asked, "How did you guys adapt to the lack of supplies?"

Seeing that Dr. Brooks was impressed with our ingenuity, I gave a brief explanation, "Well, we ate what food we could find in the houses and grocery stores in the town. Unfortunately, those resources only lasted for about a week. After the 'regular' food ran out, we resorted to eating carcasses, animal or human. You would be surprised at what desperate men will eat to survive!"

I don't think Dr. Brooks was prepared for this news! He kind of stammered and asked, "How did you, personally, cope with eating rotting flesh? Did you try to cook it somehow or just eat it as it is?"

"I was fine with it. You do what you have to do to survive. Not everyone was able to handle it. Some of the men starved to death, others ate drywall and grass, one of the guys had eaten the tips of his fingers. He only lasted about two weeks. This situation lasted for about seven months," I answered grimly.

Dr. Brooks said, "Tell me about the people that didn't survive these seven months."

I was very candid, saying, "In my opinion, they were just not ready for the worst possible situation. They thought it was going to be a cakewalk, but the situation was more of a hammer and anvil experience… and we were the piece of metal in between."

Dr. Brooks asked, "How many survived the first seven months?"

Again, I was quite candid, saying, "There were only about 850 of us left in Princeton after the first seven months. Of those that died, only 150 of them died in combat. The other 200 died of disease, starvation, and suicide."

Knowing the mental stress the survivors would have had to handle, Dr. Brooks gently pressed about it, "How did you mentally survive for those seven months?"

"My mother kept me going for the first forty-six days," I answered.

My answer indicated a tight bond that Dr. Brooks wanted to know more about. "Yeah, how so?"

I continued, "She had a quote that she told me every day before I fell asleep."

Dr. Brooks pressed, "What was the quote?"

Sharing something special about my bond with my mother was not something I did every day. Especially sharing with a person who is just 'doing his job,' but, again, for some reason, I felt as though Dr. Brooks was genuine, so I continued. "Mom always said that with the new day comes new strength and new thoughts. The quote is from Eleanor Roosevelt. After every day I would recite that quote to myself. I would also remind myself that I could survive whatever was happening to me."

Clearly pleased with himself for getting me to share a small part of my bond with my mother, Dr. Brooks continued, "That's a great quote, Gary, but what happened after those forty-six days? How did you survive for the following hundred and fifteen days?"

I knew where Dr. Brooks was taking me mentally, but I also wanted to see how I managed with the memories, so I continued. "Well, on day forty-seven I almost cracked. I almost lost my face to a hand grenade! My squad mates, Fernsby and Weppler, helped me recover by giving me a shot of adrenaline and telling me to get up. What happened next helped me stay sane."

"It was a night attack. We were holding our position at the gas station. Everyone in the inn across the street was dead. We were just three guys against the world! We were almost out of ammo. The EPC forces were closing in. We knew we were going to die if we didn't do something! Desperate people's minds go even further into survival mode!"

"Fernsby screamed at me, 'Foltz, how much do you have?!'"

"I yelled back, 'A mag and a half.'"

"'Pass me the full mag!' Fernsby called to Weppler, 'Weppler how are you doing for ammo?'"

"Weppler answered, 'About 250 rounds left!'"

"We were low on ammunition! Reality set in. We were going to die!"

"Fernsby formulated a plan by himself for himself. His plan called for him to put into action what any sane person would have considered a suicide mission. Before he left Weppler and me to die, all he said was 'Trust me, Foltz, we are going to live through this.'

"It seemed like Fernsby was gone forever! In reality, he was only gone for about an hour at the most. Weppler and I were beyond desperate. Weppler was holding a sharp stick. I was throwing shrapnel at the EPC."

"I thought it was all over until I saw the EPC forces getting shot at from the direction of the inn. You have to remember that everyone in the inn was dead. It turns out that Fernsby had grabbed the weapons and ammo off of our dead fellow soldiers and fired on the enemy. They thought we got reinforcements and retreated away from the battlefield."

Dr. Brooks was confused. "How did this keep you sane?"

I replied, "Fernsby's actions reminded me that I wasn't in this fight alone. The three of us were all fighting for the same reason."

"And what reason were you fighting for back then?" Dr. Brooks asked.

I thought that was a rather silly question, but I answered it anyway. "Freedom, peace, democracy, and for the people back home that couldn't fight but were always in my heart on the battlefield."

Dr. Brooks wanted clarification. "Who were those people, Gary?"

"My dad, Grandma, Grandpa, and my nephew Sean."

Dr. Brooks wanted a relationship clarification. "They meant a lot to you, didn't they?"

"Yes, they meant a lot to me. My nephew Sean was like a son to me."

Dr. Brooks was intrigued by my reference to Sean. "How was Sean like a son to you, Gary?"

I explained, "I taught him everything. I taught him how to walk. I taught him how to drive a car." With a smile, I added, "I even taught him proper etiquette! Sean and I walked side by side until I came to boot camp. I pretty much raised the kid by myself."

"What about the kid's mother?" queried Dr. Brooks.

I answered candidly, "She was sent over to the front lines in Africa as a heavy-duty mechanic. I haven't seen her since my brother married her."

The information about Sean and his mother seemed to placate Dr. Brooks. "That answers a lot of questions."

He continued. "Ok," to bring a conclusion to what we had been discussing, and then transitioned to our next topic. "Now, back in Princeton, after seven months of fighting, from a psychological point of view, how were you and your team doing?"

"We were deep in survival mode. We had pretty much lost any sense of our humanity in favour of cold, robotic responses. Our robotic responses were in the sense of eat, fight, sleep, repeat."

I continued, "The others didn't really show emotion. Andrews was cold as ice, Fernsby kept making jokes that the three of us ignored, and Weppler just withdrew to writing in his little book."

Dr. Brooks and I had apparently exhausted his interest in the timeframe during which our supplies did not arrive. He wanted to transition to the next time frame, namely when our supplies finally arrived. "Please, let's delve deeper into what happened on the day your unit got supplies."

"Andrews warned us to ration. 'Alright, gentlemen, don't take too much. This is what we have for a full month. We have to make due with these supplies until we get another supply drop.'

"Trying to make the best of a potentially dire situation, Fernsby tried to joke: 'Pork chow mein! Well, this is better than a communist's kidney! Hey, Weppler, am I right, or am I right?'

"Weppler chided Fernsby, 'Fernsby! Nobody found that funny.'

"Not to let Weppler steal his attempt at a little humour, misplaced or not, he said, 'Really? I thought I saw Foltz smile over there.'

"I was actually repulsed. 'Nope, that's just you, buddy.'

"Fernsby continued to defend his attempt at humour. "Well, you can't say that I didn't try.'

"'Please stop...,' said Brooks in frustration."

"'Why? Aren't I telling you the story?' I replied, somewhat perplexed."

Dr. Brooks defined what aspects of the story he wanted. "Yes, but don't tell me the story. Talk to me about the situation and the circumstances. Tell me the setting, your mood, and your emotions. Shall I go on, or do you understand what I need to know?"

Now that I knew what Dr. Brooks wanted to know, I shifted the focus. "Ok, that makes more sense. Hmmm. Let me think."

I continued, "By the time we got the supply drop, our bodies were emaciated. A good analogy would be that our bodies could be compared to a car trying to start with no gasoline. In retrospect, when we were deployed, we were soldiers. When we got back, we were animals. The conditions we endured were tortuous. The sacrifices we made were unspeakable."

Dr. Brooks tried to maintain his professionalism, but he clearly did not expect to hear what I said. "What was so unspeakable, Gary?" Undoubtedly, he felt he had helped me talk about something critical.

"Many things, but there was this one thing. Something happened that was especially heinous!" I replied. "On day eighty-two, Weppler and I were moving ammo from the church to the defensive points in the suburbs to the north."

"There were three defensive points, a restaurant, a house on the north side and a makeshift base about fifty feet off the river."

"Wait. You say there was a river?" questioned Brooks.

"Yes. Why do you ask?" I said.

Dr. Brooks pointed out, "If there was a river fifty feet away from one of your defensive points, then how come your squad mates were drinking gasoline?"

I clarified, "We tried drinking gasoline when we ran out of water in the second month. Those guys we sent out didn't even make it to the river."

Dr. Brooks apologized. "Ok. Sorry for interrupting again. Now please continue."

"Since we were moving ammo from the church to the three defensive points, we took the liberty of moving their dead and wounded. In my recollection, there were three dead and one wounded. The wounded man was a nineteen-year-old rookie suffering from a gunshot wound to his upper left body around the collarbone."

"'How serious is it, sir?' I asked the rookie's officer."

"'It's bad. He says he has had it for roughly eight days!' replied the officer."

"I found that hard to believe. 'eight days!" I asked the officer, 'How do you hide a gunshot wound for eight days?'"

"The officer replied, 'I really don't know how he hid it. He could be lying about the eight days, for all we know.'"

"Trying to be optimistic, I suggested, 'The medics might be able to do something for him…'

"The officer objected. 'No. You can't do that. His wound is too severe. It's too late to treat it with our limited supplies. Just look at him! He can barely sit up.'

"I was bewildered. 'What do we do with him then?'"

"The officer grimaced and, with a stoic look on his face, answered, 'The only humane thing we can do – put him out of his misery.'"

"I was dumbfounded! Didn't this officer understand our ammo situation? I strenuously objected, 'We can't do that! We have to save ammo. Even if it's just one bullet!'"

"The officer told me to think 'outside the box.' 'Get creative, kid! We are not limited to bullets in this town.'"

"Weppler had not been within earshot of the conversation that the officer and I had."

"'What did he say?' asked Weppler."

"'Come with me," I replied. I added, 'He told me that we have to kill him.'"

"Weppler could not believe his ears. 'What!! You have to be joking, Foltz. He's just a kid.'"

"'The officer is right, we don't have the resources to care for him and he can't be sent home.'"

"Weppler coldly challenged me. 'Alright, Foltz! How are we going to kill him?'"

"I really did not know at the time. I needed time to think."

"Later that day, we brought the kid to a Vietnamese restaurant that we cleared out. We carried him to the kitchen in the back of the restaurant. The situation got ugly, really ugly! The scene was too ugly to describe. Since we couldn't use our guns, we had to find something we could use that would have some semblance of being humane. Who were we kidding? We had a particularly gruesome job to do, and 'humane' did not really fit. All of the knives in the kitchen were either being used or were too dull to use for the task at hand. All we could find was an empty propane bottle and a dull butter knife. But what to do with them? We used what we had on hand to do what we had to do. Weppler was never the same after that day."

"How so?" asked Brooks.

Grimly, I recalled, "He used to be always interacting with everyone in the squad. He was just friendly and outgoing."

Dr. Brooks wanted a little more information. "How was Weppler different after he killed the rookie with the propane bottle?"

I explained, "He never spoke unless he needed to. He kept to himself for the rest of the mission. When he wasn't fighting, eating, or sleeping, he was writing in his little book."

"Did you ever find out what he wrote down?" pressed Dr. Brooks.

I replied, "No. Weppler always had his book on him. Nobody even bothered to ask what he was writing. We were too caught up in the war to really even think about what he was writing."

Dr. Brooks wanted to encourage me about being able to finally talk about what I had kept bottled up. "This is good. Gary. You are opening up." He now wanted another transition: "Now tell me what it was like during the last three months of your stay in Princeton."

⌐ CHAPTER 2 ¬
Strangers in the Mud

"THE LAST THREE MONTHS were the hardest; they felt like a hundred years! There were roughly 150 of us defending a fairly large town. Our supplies of food and munitions were dangerously low. Even with the odd supply drop, we were barely holding on. The town had almost been reduced to rubble. It looked like nothing could survive there, yet, miraculously, we did."

"Every night for those three months, we were attacked by drones, infantry units, artillery strikes, and the odd gas attack. If an attack could be imagined, we had to defend against it. On one of the nights, the enemy sent in a Basilisk. In fiction, a Basilisk is a giant snake whose gaze kills you instantly when it looks at you."

"The enemy's Basilisk was a drone model that looked like a snake. The drone was ten feet long and four feet high. It was made out of high-density uranium and titanium, making the drone bulletproof. It was also equipped with shotguns in its mouth, and its exterior was sharply edged. This drone was really a war machine that was designed for close combat.

"What happened that night was unforgettable! We did not have perimeter duty for a couple of hours, so we were lying on the ground trying to sleep. Suddenly, the ground started to shake, debris danced around us, and our teeth vibrated. We honestly thought the devil had come to kill us. I have since come to wish that night had been the devil. The enemy's Basilisk drone shot up through the ground, ripping apart the man beside me in the blink of an eye. The drone tore through our defensive strong points like a hot knife slicing through butter.

"We fought that Basilisk for what seemed like a lifetime! In reality, the battle lasted only a few hours. When we finally disabled the drone, we did man and ammo counts. We counted sixty casualties and forty dead. We used over half of our ammo to stop it from massacring the rest of us. That drone had cost us dearly! Of the original hundred and fifty men, we were now roughly fifty able-bodied men. Having sixty casualties, we had no choice but to assign fourteen men to care for them. This included the medics."

"We now had all of thirty-six men to hold off the next day's attack. We had to defend differently. We had to come up with a different strategy. Knowing that we would be crippled of manpower, the enemy brought in four strings. The enemy thought we would be exhausted and disheartened. They thought we would have nothing left to live for.

"Please let me stop you there," interjected Brooks. Then he asked, "What is a string?"

I continued, "In the weaponized drone world, there are a couple of terms that are unique. One of those terms is 'bead.' The other is 'string.' A bead is a drone the size of a pacifier, with small blades that spin around the outside. Ten beads can cut a car perfectly in half. There can be any number of beads in a string. Each of the strings that were coming our way looked like there were about a thousand beads in it. There were roughly four thousand of them coming for the thirty-six of us. Four thousand beads coming after thirty-six men! The enemy meant business and they wanted the battle over quickly. Needless to say, the battle turned really ugly, really fast."

"Please continue, you were saying something about…" Dr. Brooks paused and looked at his notes. He looked up and said, "Nothing left to live for?"

"Precisely! Yes. The enemy believed we were physically and mentally incapacitated," I replied.

"Were they correct to some degree?" Dr. Brooks questioned.

"The enemy was partially right – we were exhausted and disheartened. But when hardened men are stripped of their humanity, if they still have something left to live for, they become desperate. The enemy had stripped us of our humanity, but they had not succeeded in destroying our something to live for – our will to survive. The enemy had made us desperate, and desperate men who still have that will to survive are savage. That was the one day we were not men – we were savage beasts!"

"Explain the battle, Gary. What was it like fighting those beads and strings?" asked Dr. Brooks. He was pleased with himself for referring to the terms I had just explained.

"Well, anti-drone weapons, EMP grenades and small explosives are the most effective weapons to neutralize beads. The trouble was that you need enough weapons, and enough men to operate them, to have a fighting chance. We did not have enough of either to have that fighting chance. There were just so many of these things… we were overrun in a matter of minutes! Friends beside me got ripped apart in seconds. The odds were clearly stacked against us! We could barely hold our ground with our limited weaponry and manpower. When the drones broke through our defenses, they got to the gas station and the inn in less than five minutes. Everyone in the gas station and the inn was massacred in seconds.

"I looked at Fernsby and rhetorically said, 'You got any jokes to get us through this one?'

"Fernsby just looked at me. He didn't respond; he didn't even smile. This was the only time I saw him like this. He looked like he had lost the will to survive. That was the moment I lost all hope that I would get home safely.

"Fighting the beads was another level of warfare. Men's bodies were being dismembered and disembowelled, and their skulls were being shattered in a matter of seconds. We were barely holding them back. I truly believed I was a dead man walking. I believed I was going to die in the blood of strangers in the mud.

"I almost gave up. Then I remembered a promise I gave to my brother: that I would take care of his son Sean. I stood up and fought with all the fight I had left in me. After fighting for hours on end, the strings fell back. We had lived to fight another day. Even more important than living to fight another day, we had saved over fifty lives."

"Why does that matter to you, Gary?" questioned Brooks.

I replied, "It was the first time in the war I had identified exactly what I was fighting for."

"You didn't know what you were fighting for when you were conscripted?" Brooks asked incredulously.

"No," I replied rather defensively. "I didn't know what I was fighting for." I continued rather bitterly, "All I thought was that my country was sending me to fight someone else's war."

Doubting my story, Brooks questioned me further. "How could you not know what you were fighting for? Clearly you were defending your country on its own soil."

Wryly, I continued, "Yes. But for every war there is a reason why it started, and I still don't know why the EPC was attacking everybody."

Dr. Brooks back-pedalled a bit. "Alright, that's a fair point to make." He wanted to transition and shift the focus. "Ok. Tell me how the very end of your stay in Princeton was."

I was actually relieved to have the focus shifted. "We still had two days before we would be evacuated. There were about sixty of us. At mid-day there was a thick fog setting in. Fernsby and I were in a crater on the street, up to our knees in a black sludge."

"'Do you have any idea what this black stuff is?' Fernsby asked me."

"In full disgust, I retorted, 'Not a clue! But you are welcome to taste it to find out.'

"Not to be outdone by my disgust, Fernsby said sarcastically, 'You know, since I can definitely smell blood and machine oil at the same time, I think I'll take a pass on that one.'

"Dripping with sarcasm, I replied, 'All I can say is that you are most definitely missing out.'

"'I would beg to differ.' Fernsby quipped.

"Suddenly, Fernsby snapped his head away and said. 'Did you hear that?'

"'Hear what?' I questioned.

"'Pass me those binoculars.' Fernsby whispered urgently, reaching for the binoculars as he spoke. He grabbed them from me and looked through them.

"'What do you see?' I questioned.

"'Nothing! That's strange. I swear I heard something,' Fernsby said nervously.

"Next thing we knew we were getting shot at from multiple directions. Our crater in the street that had seemed safe enough just moments ago was now looking like it was going to be our grave.

"Fernsby and I looked at each other in despair. We both felt as though our survivor luck had just run out. What did we do then? How could we survive this barrage of gunfire? Then the unimaginable happened! The shooting stopped, seemingly for no reason. A man dressed in a suit of military grade armour appeared out of the fog. His suit had the word 'Valkyrie' printed on his chest. The man simply said, 'Your uncle sends his regards.' Then he extended his wings and flew away into the fog.

"'Who on earth is your uncle?' questioned Fernsby incredulously.

The very real memory took me mentally back to that crater in the street. I still had trouble believing what had happened there. I absent-mindedly shook my head and replied, "He's a field doctor in Europe. I didn't know how he was in touch with the Hyenas."

My answer took Dr. Brooks by surprise. He pressed, "The Hyenas? Who are the Hyenas?"

"They are a group of mercenaries that run around in those suits and do the dirty work for governments. The mercs were neutral in the war." Then I realized that Dr. Brooks had not done his job. I sternly looked at him. "Did you even *look* at your combat manual?"

Dr. Brooks took my question poorly. "Come on, Gary! Does it look like I read the combat manual?"

I replied, "Well, that Hyena's suit was Valkyrie class. A Valkyrie suit class is mainly designed for aerial combat up to 40,000 feet."

Dr. Brooks tried to lighten the conversation. "Man, you are a nerd!" Then he continued, "Did you study the combat manual?"

"No. Not the whole book. I just skipped to the end and read the important things. I read about the Hyena suit classes Valkyrie, Minotaur, Hippogriff, Siren, and Draugr."

Then, in more of a challenge than a question, I said, "Shall I continue?"

"No. I think that's enough of a history lesson for today, Mr. Foltz."

I continued the next day. "When we went back to resupply, the school was burning. Andrews was pulling Weppler out of a pile of rubble. All of our provisions and ammo were gone. The grim reality was that all we had to survive on for the next two days was what we had on our belts and what we could find on our dead.

"'Andrews! What happened?!' questioned Fernsby.

"I thought that Fernsby was out of line. Andrews was our officer, but it sounded like Fernsby was verbally demanding an answer from him."

"'The Hyenas! They are what happened. A Draugr suit and a Minotaur suit just strolled up and shot everything to smithereens,' said Andrews, 'with little worry or fear.' Then he added, 'Not exactly certain how we survived!'

"'How's Weppler holding up?' I asked.

"'Minor cuts and bruises all around,' Andrews replied.

"'So he will be fine for tomorrow?' Fernsby asked hopefully.

"'Well, he looks fine to me,' Andrews answered, 'but I'm not a medic.' Then, narrowing his eyes and focussing on Weppler's leg, he said, 'What's that sticking through your leg?'

"Weppler answered, 'I think that's a piece of rebar, or my leg is broken. And that." Weppler said, pointing at something protruding from his pant leg, "that's a bone."

"'Let's just leave it there. Just in case it is bone. Fernsby, find us a chair for Weppler before he tries anything stupid,' commanded Andrews.

I continued my story for Brooks. "We tied off his wound and put him in a wheelchair. The wheelchair only had three wheels, but it was something for Weppler to sit on. Then we scavenged for supplies and prepared for our last stand in and around the church.

"It was about midday. I was in a group of four men, including myself. Two of us, Baines and I, were tasked to guard the other two men, who were our only mortar crew. In addition to guarding the crew, Baines and I had to defend against the enemy for as long as we could. Those hours were the longest, toughest, and most gruesome of my life.

"The town had become little more than a catacomb to hide dead men's bodies. We knew that our bodies could be added to that catacomb that day, but we also knew, as we dug deep into ourselves, we weren't going down without a fight!

"The fighting during that time started with a green flare to the west. After the flare fired, it was soon followed by tear gas. The gas encased the battlefield. We didn't have a way to counter the gas, so we just had to tough it out. But what followed up would be what almost killed us."

"What was it? What almost killed you, Foltz?" Brooks pressed urgently.

"I don't know. I didn't see it... I heard it," I said. I still could hardly believe that I had not seen what almost killed us.

"Describe to me what you heard," Dr. Brooks encouraged.

"What I heard sounded like death itself. Cold. Lifeless. Not human or man-made... not of this world," I said in slight confusion.

Dr. Brooks wanted to shift focus and asked softly, "Please tell me what happened after the thing massacred everyone else at your post?"

"After everyone else at my post was massacred, the fog cleared. Two attack helicopters came in to kill the rest of us. I tried to get in contact with the air defense station. I got no response. What to do now?! I had to get innovative... creative! I motioned Fernsby to the surface-to-air bazookas to take out the helicopters; my job was to distract them from shooting at Fernsby.

"I went over to our mortar pit. I grabbed as many mortar shells as I could carry. I went back to my post and threw a shell in the direction of the helicopters. I attempted to shoot the mortar shell while it was still in the air but missed. I repeated throwing and shooting many times before I got lucky and actually shot the shell in mid-air. The resulting explosion did nothing to the helicopters. Fortunately, my plan wasn't to disable the helicopters. I just wanted to distract them enough to lure the helicopters away from Fernsby. Was I being creative or just foolish? I could care less! The plan HAD to work. The plan was our only chance at survival.

"When I ran out of mortar shells to throw at them, I ran behind what used to be a cement wall. I could only hope that I had bought Fernsby enough time. Our plan was designed to save the lives of all those who were hiding from the helicopters, not just the lives of Fernsby and myself. All of our lives depended on us doing our jobs in the face of almost certain death."

"'Fernsby! What the hell is taking you so long!?" I screamed while the helicopter's guns were effortlessly tearing through my cover.

"'Just give me a second. It takes a while to load this thing," said Fernsby calmly. While I was pleased that Fernsby sounded calm, right now it just did not seem appropriate!

"'It's a bazooka! You put the rocket in the back, lock it in place, and pull the trigger!' I screamed with even more urgency, as the helicopter guns were pretty much destroying my cover.

"'Yeah, but which side is the back?' Fernsby's calmness was starting to erode.

"'Thinking it should be rather obvious, I angrily shouted, 'There should be a place labelled 'load here.'

"'Oh yeah! There it is!' I could hear Fernsby was pleased with himself for figuring the gun out. "

"A few moments later the helicopters fell burning from the sky. Fernsby had saved my life once again, and I was more than happy to admit it. We thought we were past the worst of it, but we were wrong. We were so very, very wrong! We had only survived the beginning of the onslaught! We had another challenge bearing down on us, seemingly from the pit of Hell itself!

"I didn't even know what was attacking us until one of the beasts jumped over a wall and ripped a guy to pieces with its jaws. The beasts were called Brutes! Think of the biggest dog you have ever seen, oversize it, and then make it out of reinforced steel. Each of the Brutes had loaded machine guns and rocket launchers on its back. About four of them were coming at us. We were all out of position. We were being slaughtered. None of us knew how long we fought. I just knew I was very lucky to be able to walk away from the fight.

"Even though it seemed like the EPC attacked us in every way possible, we soon found out they still had new tactics available. With just thirty minutes left before our reinforcements arrived, the EPC forces hit us with over two hundred fully armed soldiers. There were only twelve of us left. Our only hope of survival was to get one of those mechanized Brutes back online. Since all our engineers were dead, I was the next best thing to an engineer. Andrews tasked us to get one of those Brutes back online.

"From my memory of learning weaponized robotics, I had to make sure three parts were working on the Brute: the CPU, mobility parts, and the sensors. Since I didn't have the time to put new parts on a Brute, I had to use the one that needed minimal repairs, which was in the middle of the street behind a car, or what looked like it could have been a car.

"There was still a bit of work to be done. The CPU was fried and some of the sensors were cracked. I had to run around to find the other disabled Brutes and collect from them what I needed. Andrews, Fernsby, and I split up to find the other Brutes. I heard that one of them was down by a house on the northwest side of town, precisely where the EPC forces were attacking from!

"When I found the Brute, my fellow soldiers were using it for cover against enemy fire. 'I heard you are looking for parts for a Brute to get it back up and running,' said a soldier.

"'Yes, I am,' I answered, 'but I have a slight problem with this one,' I cautioned.

"'What's your problem?' the soldier asked.

"I explained, 'I can see that the sensors on this one are worse than the one we have back there.' I motioned behind me. 'But there is a chance the CPU still works. For me to repair the one I am working on with parts from this one, I need to be in the open.'

"'What? What are you saying?' the soldier asked, clearly not expecting my answer.

"'I need you guys to cover me while I cut this Brute open,' I explained.

"The soldier strenuously objected. 'That's suicide!'

"I looked the soldier in the eye, put my hand on his shoulder, and countered. I had to tell him the truth. 'It's the only way!'

I continued my story to Dr. Brooks. "I did not wait to debate with the soldier. Time was slipping away. I vaulted over the crippled Brute and proceeded to cut with my makeshift blowtorch. I only needed a few minutes. I wasn't even sure if I was cutting in the right place. As soon as I started cutting, I discovered that the Brute's armoured exterior was damaged, making it cut faster. I finished the cutting fairly quickly. I found the CPU was perfectly intact. I grabbed it and vaulted back over the Brute for cover."

"'Alright, boys, I am done. Come back,' I said.

"None of them came back with me. All I heard was one of them saying, 'Kid, this idea better work! Those men died to make sure the rest of us survived.'

I continued my story for Brooks. "But my job wasn't done yet. I still needed to find intact sensors so the Brute could see. Without the sensors for vision, the Brute would be useless."

"Fernsby's Brute was in pieces. What else could go wrong? We soon found out! I made my way over to Andrew's Brute. It had been decapitated, and the head weighed over two hundred pounds. There was no way we could move it. It was at the bottom of the riverbank on the southeast side of town. I had to get there fast because our front line on the west side wasn't going to hold back the enemy forever. I ran as fast as I could, as our lives depended on it. I had to run across an open field to get to Andrews. I knew that if I died, everyone would know that I died giving my all.

"I ran about fifteen feet when I got shot in the left shoulder. I ignored the pain and ran about another twenty feet. Another bullet hit me in the shin. I couldn't run anymore but I wouldn't give up. I forced my body into a crippled, limping, mass and kept going. I pushed through the pain shooting all across my body. Right before I got to Andrews, I got shot again, in the back of my other shoulder.

"Despite the pain I was in, I could see the Brute's head at the bottom of the hill, at the base of the riverbank. I had to get down to that hunk of metal. I tried to limp down the hill, but my limp turned into a stumble, which sent me rolling down the hill. I broke a couple of fingers, a wrist, some ribs, and cracked my skull. Despite my gunshot wounds and broken bones, I was, very unexpectedly, still able to move and extract the sensors from the Brute's head.

"It took a while to get back up to the top of the hill, but when I finally got up there, Andrews was sitting on a pile of bricks, crying. 'Sir, why are you crying?' I asked.

"'It's over, Foltz. Our reinforcements are here! Foltz, we can... go... home.' The relief he was experiencing was so intense his body shook and he spoke with a slight stutter.

"'What? How?' I responded to Andrews's news with disbelief. I continued talking more *to* than *with* Andrews. 'I was down there for less than five minutes, and support isn't supposed to be here for another few hours!'

"Andrews explained with a smile in his voice, 'Turns out our American friends from the south decided to skip breakfast.'

"I looked behind myself and saw helicopters and tanks rolling in, with infantry not so far behind. Our two-year nightmare was over. Andrews and I were directed to the evacuation helicopter, where they took a head count.

"There were only five of us left: Andrews, Fernsby, Weppler, a guy named Colson, and myself. We were all awarded the Victorian Cross when we got back home. Our division refers to us as the Unshakable Five. I carry that title with great humility."

"Why do you say that, Gary?" questioned Brooks.

With a great deal of pent-up maliciousness, I blurted out, "People gave that title to us like it was a present, or something we strove for. They have no idea the horrors we experienced. People kept telling me I did such a great thing. They made it sound like the horrors actually came out of a comic book. Let me tell you, nothing that happened was even remotely relatable to a comic book!"

I continued, "I barely slept for the first two weeks I was home in the hospital. My body simply could not relax. My brain was still very much in survival mode. My brain kept telling my body that I had to go on watch in the next few hours."

Dr. Brooks wanted to settle me down somehow and said, "I think you are overreacting about this."

I could not believe what Brooks was saying! "Really!! You think I'm overreacting? This is me controlling myself with a self-control I did not think I had." A new wave of spite started to take over. "Hell, I haven't even told you the worst parts of my story yet."

"Well," Dr. Brooks cautioned, "if you can control your emotions, we can continue."

I swallowed hard and took a couple of deep breaths. I continued. "Ok, I will try to keep myself in check."

Brooks cautioned me again. "Good. Can we now continue without trouble?"

I could feel that I was regaining control of my emotions. "Yes, we can."

Satisfied with my reassurance, he encouraged me. "Ok. Please continue."

"When we got back to base, we did not receive any fanfare at all. We were bewildered. We felt like our nightmare had never happened. No one greeted us. No one shook our hands. No one even said so much as hello. The closest thing we had to a greeting came from the medics who were doing first aid on us. We felt isolated. The only person, other than the medics, who spoke to us was, I thought, a Special Forces agent."

"'Hey guys, kudos to you for holding that town for so long. The Americans depended on you to make an advance on the western front,' said the agent.

"'Thanks?' I said with uncertainty. 'We were never told that!'

"The agent continued, 'You seem lost right now. I will come back later when you fellas have your bearings.'

"'Ok. See you later, I guess.' I was not certain if the agent was trying to tell me something or if I was just being paranoid.

"The five of us were sent back to the hospital in Edmonton for recuperation and rehabilitation. My wounds and pitifully poor health made both quite challenging. I wasn't able to walk properly for four months.

"About a week after I started walking, the agent came back. I was resting on my bed when he arrived in my area of the hospital. When he got to my bed, he observed, 'You look better than the last time I saw you. Good on you!' He continued, 'Are you well enough to take a short walk?'

"Curiosity got the better of me, so I asked him, 'Can I at least know your name before we walk?'

"The agent answered without hesitation. 'I'm Agent Whittle. I am with the CIA, Foreign Operations Division.'

"I now felt slightly safer but was wondering why he was talking to me. I didn't trust him… he would have to earn my trust. "Sure, I could go for a walk." I immediately got off the bed, and Whittle and I went for a walk in the hospital.

"Once again, curiosity got the better of me and I blurted out, 'Ok, Whittle, why are we speaking today? What do you want?!'

"Whittle answered, 'Well, Mr. Foltz, you and your team did a great deed for your country. Your country's military leaders have decided to promote your team to Canada's first Lion Skin Division.'

"I had no idea what that meant, so I asked him, 'Well, that sounds great, but can you please tell me what a Lion Skin Division is?'

"Whittle continued, 'Well, the Canadian Government has been working on a new type of super soldier. You see, once you guys get combat ready in a few weeks, you are going to have a chance to be a part of history again.'

"MANY, many questions started flooding my brain, but the most crucial question was how many of 'you guys' we would be. 'Is it just the five of us doing this?'

"'Oh no!' Whittle was almost relieved that the size of our team was foremost in my concerns. He continued, 'There are over five hundred people on the list, including myself and my team of about a hundred and twenty men and women.'

"I began to wonder why Whittle was talking to me instead of Andrews. After all, Andrews was our officer, so I told him, 'You should be talking to Andrews about this, not me.'

"The agent answered my concern quite matter-of-factly. "Andrews will take another month to be ready. We start the new project in three weeks. In light of this predicament, we have chosen you to be the lead officer. You have your choice of the hundred men and women to join you. I will give you some time to decide. I hope to hear from you soon."

"I didn't know what to do. Did I accept and recruit, or not? I knew my team and I would be sent to a battlefield somewhere. The details were very vague. I talked to my squadmates about it. I found out that everyone, except Colson, had absolutely NO interest in joining the team. I had my answer for Whittle, or, rather, we had our answer for him: a big fat thanks but no thanks!

"I told Whittle I was turning down his offer. The four of us just waited until we were combat ready. When we were combat ready, we were assigned to the Royal 22nd Rifle Regiment – the men we relieved from Princeton two years before.

"We were sent to the army base in Edmonton to rendez-vous with the rest of the regiment. Captain UmBach was our commanding officer."

CHAPTER 3

The Math Behind the War

I T WAS AN INTERESTING experience being under the command of Captain UmBach. If chess were the battlefield, Captain UmBach would be the old man who always beats you, no matter how many tricks you have up your sleeve. He would predict his opponent's movements from the first move to checkmate.

Many times I wondered why UmBach wasn't one of the top generals in the army. In my opinion, UmBach should have been commanding thousands. But then, the military's ranking system did not answer to me. The military needs masters of the soft, personal skills to deal with people, and to most effectively manage them.

The military also needs masters of math and robotics to give soldiers the tools they need. Math and robotics, cold hard skills, are my specialties. I thoroughly enjoy working with things that have unforgiving rules on how they work.

When my team and I got to the field base in the Yukon, we were told that we were going to be working with the Americans to push the enemy back into Alaska. This is when I met the Handmaiden.

The term 'Handmaiden' was one that Brooks had not heard before, and he could hardly ask, "Who is this Handmaiden?" quickly enough.

"She is a Delta Force operative," I continued. "She possesses skills and intelligence that few other soldiers I have ever fought beside could claim. When we fought together, she always handled herself with efficiency and professionalism, ALWAYS had my six and there were many times I simply regarded her as 'one of the guys.'"

Brooks wanted to know more about why I held her in high esteem. "Tell me how you two met."

"We met after the first briefing in the Yukon. I had gone to the gun range to better my aim. It was raining outside. I was alone in the range before she came in. In keeping with her professionalism, she was very distant. She was tired of men trying to talk to her simply because she is a woman."

Knowingly or not, and whether she wanted to talk or not, I had an urge to talk to her that I couldn't ignore, so I tried to get her attention. All I had to do was get her to look at me, and I had to get her to say something – anything – personal to me. Now, remember, this was happening BEFORE I knew what she was all about.

"I saw you in the briefing room. Are you excited to get a real win in this liquidation that the generals call war?" I questioned.

She slowly turned her head to me with mass confusion on her face. Then she turned her head back and said, "Yep." Her focus was again on her weapon and down the range. I could tell she was trying to be polite, but the word 'liquidation' distracted her from her practice.

Well, I did get a word – one word - out of her. The word was strictly polite, but it was a word. I was very bored at that time so I wanted to get a little bit more from her. I wanted to spark conversation, any conversation. Thinking back, I now realize that I had put her in a very awkward position. She just wanted to be left alone to work on her aim, but she found herself in a room with a guy whose testosterone was flowing and was using her for target practice simply because she is a woman. She must have wanted to shoot me right there on the spot!

"I fought down in BC for two years in a town called Princeton. All I have seen in this war is how to defend. I really want to see what the attacking side is like… have you ever been on the attacking side of a battle?"

"Yep." She was still very focussed on her weapon and her aim and was very clearly trying to ignore me.

That 'yep' was different somehow. Was I getting through that professionalism? Getting through to the woman? I really wanted to keep talking to her, but she really didn't want to talk to me, I could tell. Should I try something a little more personal and see what happens, I wondered? Yes! Let's see what happens…

"I didn't get your name. I am Master Corporal Foltz. But you can call me Gary… What's your name?"

Well, I had given the game my all. How was she going to respond? How quickly would she respond? Would she ever speak to me again? Man, I was just an idiot! The stupid things testosterone makes men do. If she spoke to me again without disgust, the testosterone would make me feel like a He-Man ready to strut my stuff – whatever 'stuff' that may be.

Then it happened. In one action she lifted her head and trained her eyes on me. The look in her eyes was one of disgust. Her facial muscles were tensed. Whatever she was going to say, she was going to say it once, and I had better get it correct. "Gary, I come to the gun range to be alone and not be bothered. Can you just stop bothering me, please?"

Well, she was as polite as she could be and still be professional, while basically telling me to shut up and leave her alone. I now felt kind of foolish for letting my inner man control me like I was an animal. Well, let's face it – that was precisely how I had acted! My bad!

Licking my battle wounds, I sheepishly attempted both an apology and a tip to help her hit the target. "Sorry, I will leave you be. Just to let you know, with this torrential rain, the humidity will make it easier to shoot during long-distance engagements."

She replied, "Thanks for the tip, rookie."

Our first encounter was a bit precarious, to say the least.

That evening, our squads were organized into teams. As luck would have it, she and I were put on the same team. Our team was tasked with disabling the communications our enemy had constructed after they set up their field base in North Alaska. We soon found out that we were not fighting human soldiers!

"What, or whom, were you fighting?" asked Brooks.

"They were droids. Combat droids. Combat droids designed to be the ultimate killing machine," I answered.

Brooks was intrigued! "Can you give me more specifics on these droids?"

I explained, "They were called CB8 Mark 14 in our combat manuals. That was too much to say, so we nicknamed them droids." With a smirk, I added, "Worked for us."

Brooks realized he wanted more than a name. "These droids, what were they capable of? What did they look like??"

Brooks wanted to know just how technically advanced the droids were. I assured him that they were mid-level. "They were not top of the line, but they could still deal out a sizable amount of damage. Some of us even referred to them like they were supernatural."

Since the droids' physical appearance reasonably resembled the human body, we could concentrate on what we would consider to be weak points on the human body, such as the shoulders, kneecaps, neck, and jaw. You had to focus on those points to win the fight; after you broke through the armour, of course.

Brooks was clearly excited to learn that a regular soldier could defeat a machine that was capable of taking down a war machine. He blurted out, "How *did* you fight them?" almost unintelligibly.

I slipped into kind of a teaching mode, which made me feel good because I was teaching this over-educated doctor something that he could not fathom! "First, you have to penetrate their armour. Then you have to find and exploit their weak points. While we had a strategy, the odds were against us.

There were over twenty droids and only six of us. We needed a plan that would work!"

My team was discussing how to take out the droids most efficiently without raising an alarm. We were stuck in terms of how to execute our objective. Then the Handmaiden entered the room and, not so subtly, demonstrated her intelligence.

"Ok, have you guys come up with a plan yet?" Handmaiden asked.

I figured that she had a plan but did not want to step on people's toes, at least not just yet!

"Nope. Not even close!" replied Andrews in a manner that implied the men of the team had better things to do than entertain the whimsical thinking of a *woman*.

Handmaiden was losing patience! We did not have time to debate, and she knew it. "Oh, come on now! Think!" She continued, "These droids have night vision; they have thermal vision, and they have x-ray vision. We have to go in when those advantages are nullified. So, how do we nullify those advantages?? *THINK*! You have to think outside the box. That's how you won in Princeton. You guys thought outside the box for two years and faced worse than a few dozen droids!"

Andrews was getting quite defensive. He focussed on her and challenged her. "Ok, sweetheart, what didn't we think of?"

He was letting being questioned interfere with his thinking. For a soldier to let anyone or anything interfere with thinking is a cardinal sin. To make matters worse, for him, he was letting a woman interfere!

Handmaiden, using as much patience as she could, knelt down, grabbed some sealed packages from the supplies boxes, stood back up, looked Andrews in the eye, and asked him, "Andrews, have you ever heard of active camouflage?"

Andrews heard every bit of her sarcasm aimed directly, and only, at him. Perhaps Handmaiden was wrong to verbally and visually aim her sarcasm at him, but she had a point to make and precious little time to do it.

Andrews quickly recovered enough to throw her sarcasm right back at her. He narrowed his eyes, stared Handmaiden down, and, with pursed lips, retorted, "I heard that we are about eight years away from coming out with a prototype."

For a split second, Handmaiden looked like she enjoyed Andrews's comeback. I think she enjoyed seeing that Andrews *could* think on his feet! Still holding the sealed packages in her hand, and now extending her hand toward Andrews as if to make a point, she said, "Well, Andrews, these aren't suits. They are homemade active camo ponchos. I know a guy in engineering. He sent us these for testing."

Handmaiden's clarification confused Andrews. With attitude and a smirk, he asked her, "So, we are wearing prototypes of a prototype! We *are* going to die!"

Handmaiden replied immediately, saying, "This is better than going in with just our gear on."

Handmaiden's confidence in her plan was winning Andrews over. He quickly conceded and asked, "So, what's the plan?"

Handmaiden answered, "Our ground team is going to be wearing these Mylar ponchos equipped with nail files in them."

Her answer confused Andrews, as, I am sure, it confused the rest of our team.

Andrews couldn't contain his curiosity. "How is that going to work?"

Straight to the point, Handmaiden explained, "Mylar reflects the thermal. The nail files will mess with their x-ray vision. Attacking just after sunrise will render the night vision useless. They will have to fight you without visual enhancements."

Handmaiden had just clearly demonstrated her intelligence in a situation where clear thinking was required. Hers was also the only plan we had on countering the droids without being seen.

Since sunrise would be at 0700 hours and the main force were to attack at 1300 hours, we had about five hours to infiltrate, sabotage, and evacuate without being seen. Our plan seemed easy and straightforward. Our plan seemed too good to be true! Wait a minute! What do they say things that seem just too good to be true usually are? Shortly, we were going to find out just how poor the battlefield intelligence was!

⌐ CHAPTER 4 ¬
The Blind Spot

FROM OUR INTELLIGENCE SOURCES, we knew what resources the enemy had. They consisted of a few hundred droids, some light tanks, and about forty human officers. Unfortunately, there was no way for us to know how they would be deployed. We had to push forward even though we were drastically outmatched.

Brooks wanted the whole story. "Tell me what happened from beginning to end; from the second you left base to the end of the fighting that day." To emphasize accuracy, he added, "Take your time if you need to."

I momentarily collected my thoughts and then calmly dove into the story.

"Our team left the field base at 0600 hours. At first, the team occupied two vehicles. In the lead vehicle were Fernsby,

Weppler, Andrews, and myself. Following in the second car were Handmaiden with her team."

"At 0730 hours, my team got out of our transport and started on foot. Handmaiden's team drove to the overwatch position, which was about thirty minutes away from where our vehicle was parked. We hiked for an hour. By the time we were all in position and ready to disable the communications camp, we only had about three hours to execute our plan. Failure to execute our plan was really not an option. If we failed to execute, we would lose Yukon and probably the northern front in Canada. There was a lot of pressure on us to succeed in this operation," I said.

"Please continue," Dr. Brooks encouraged.

"My team was about ten yards away from the communications tent when we heard a noise in the tent. There was someone in the tent! Someone being *in* the tent changed everything. We had to up our game, and up it silently. We were going to have to take him out without noise, and everything was dead silent!"

"Andrews, what are we going to do about this guy?" I whispered.

"Well, not to be blunt, but we can go to the other side, wire it with C4, and blow it up," Andrews whispered back.

I volunteered to ask Handmaiden. "Let me get on comms and ask Handmaiden if she is on board with blowing it up."

Andrews objected. "No! I am sick and tired of taking orders from that woman. Let's blow this place to kingdom come!"

I was really not in favour of all the quick attention I figured we would get from the enemy by blowing the communications setup to smithereens, but at the same time, Andrews had struck a chord with me about taking orders from Handmaiden. Maybe in this circumstance it would be better to apologize for all the noise than to ask permission to cause all the noise!

When we were done running around the camp, rigging it to blow, we got away to a safe distance. Andrews gave me the detonator, saying, "Foltz, I bestow you the honour of blowing this place sky high."

I took the detonator and pressed the button. As the explosives detonated the communications camp, I felt relieved. Feeling relieved from destroying the camp kind of surprised me because we were there deliberately to destroy the camp.

"What exactly were you relieved of, Gary?" asked Brooks.

"Relieved of finally feeling like we were winning the war," I replied. Deep down I was fully aware that destroying the camp really did not have that much of an overall impact on the war, but just saying it gave me a sense of accomplishment.

"This first session has been very eye-opening for me, Gary. Unfortunately, we have run out of time."

"It's already been an hour?" I asked incredulously.

"Well, you know what they say: time flies when you are in the place you are meant to be. I will see you next Tuesday at four p.m., I presume?"

"Yes. Next Tuesday at four p.m.," I confirmed.

As I was driving back to my house, I started to speculate. Why did I survive? My friends, most of my family, and fellow soldiers were all gone. Why did I survive? There had to be a reason. Could the underlying reason that I was the last man standing just be dumb luck?

When I got home, the hour was very late. My dad was sitting at the kitchen table with his hands folded. The scene made me think he was waiting for me.

"Hey, Dad, what keeps you up so late?" I asked. I was momentarily tempted to add a little one-liner with a chuckle, but something stopped me at the last instant.

My dad replied simply, "I was worried about you. I wanted to make sure you got home safe."

I wanted to lighten the mood a little, so I replied with a soft smile and soft voice, "Well, thanks for that. As you can see, I did make it home safe. You can go to bed now."

My dad was not done, though. He stood up, walked over to the fridge, grabbed a photo, and approached me with it.

"You kind of remind me of your mother, Gary. You, like her, are kind and strong willed. You never put your own priorities ahead of someone else's. I have also lost both of you to war." Dad's posture drooped a little, and his voice softened with an angry hurt. "The list doesn't stop with you two. This war has also taken Oliver, Brian, Kira, Thomas, and Ethan. They are all gone because of this god-forsaken war that should never have happened. I know you don't remember, Gary, but, believe it or not, there was a time when there was peace in this world. There was a time when there were no guns being shot, nobody died from military action, and everyone was treated equally.

"I should have volunteered to fight in Europe when the EPC invaded in 2032. Plant workers were not allowed to volunteer to fight because we were needed to keep production of war machines at the plant at a steady rate. So we could keep our men in the front lines equipped and ready to fight the enemy."

In a vain attempt to help Dad remember I was still with him, I said, "Dad, you didn't lose me. I'm right here. I am safe in our home." Somehow I knew I did not know the full story.

Dad continued, "I haven't lost you, at least not yet! I guess you haven't seen your mail yet. After you are done with Dr. Brooks, they are sending you back."

"Dad, you are freaking me out. I am not leaving for a long time. I am not physically ready to be sent back." Then, on an adrenaline rush, I added, "Besides, you don't need to worry about me! I can take care of myself." I did not let on, but I would not have blamed Dad for not believing that last statement, because I didn't really believe it myself.

With bitterness in his voice and on his face, Dad said, "That is exactly what your mother said before leaving for Europe thirty-one years ago. Do you know what happened to her Gary?"

"Yes. I remember she was in the field hospital. The field hospital was bombed by artillery fire. She survived the bombing only to die in a hospital in Ukraine a few weeks later. Dad, you can't hang on to the past. The past will only weigh you down. The best you can do is to grieve for all you have lost until the tears stop, accept what happened, and then move on. If you stick yourself to the past, you won't have a future. But that's on you to decide – live in the past with all its hurt and trauma or live for the future with its adventure to be experienced."

I gave Dad a gentle hug to tell him that my intent was to encourage him, but his whole demeanour was one of defeat. I slowly walked away and went to bed.

As I thought about our conversation, I realized it was the most that Dad and I had spoken in the past nineteen years. It felt pleasant but also defective and sad at the same time. My dad seemed so distant, despite being right in front of me.

As I lay in bed falling asleep, I started thinking that I was supposed to survive the war, a war I had fought in for eleven years. That same war was still in full conflict. Neither side was showing any inclination of wanting the war to end. I kept questioning myself:

- How does a teacher survive when seasoned soldiers don't?
- How does that teacher walk away after the mission?
- Why does everyone call that teacher a hero just because he survived?

Dreamland was calling, and I succumbed.

CHAPTER 5
Terrain

CLEARLY PLEASED TO SEE me again, Dr. Brooks asked, "Hey Gary, how have you been for the past week?"

Honesty is always the best policy, so I answered truthfully, "To be honest, the past week has been quite boringly repetitive."

Brooks wanted more information, so he asked for it. "Yeah? Please elaborate."

I obliged him. "Well, every day I wake up at eight, have a shower, eat breakfast, go for a run, and then come back home and wait for my dad to come home. When my dad does get home, at eleven p.m., I try to strike up a constructive conversation with him. Each day I promise myself that I am going to do everything I can to have a different conversation with him. But my dad's focus is always on complaining about the war that's still going on overseas!"

I paused for a minute and then voiced an observation that just occurred to me. "You know, Dr. Brooks, my dad has never asked me how I have been since I have come back." I had never vocalized that thought before, and hearing it saddened me a little. Then another thought snuck into my head that kind of surprised me a little as well. " Dr. Brooks, I honestly don't feel like he even cares about how I've been!"

Ever the head doctor, Brooks wanted to explore my last statement a little. "How does that make you feel?"

Almost before I had a chance to mentally filter my response, I blurted out, "I feel abandoned and alone. I feel like I am still in Princeton."

"Gary, coming back to society, after what you've been through, and being expected to function as though your experiences never happened, is absolutely unfair. But that's what society expects. Soldiers are expected to protect established society. Society expects soldiers to endure absolute horrors. Society expects soldiers to just deal with their lives and then come out smiling on the other end. And, if the soldier can't come out smiling, that soldier is weak and defective – not worthy of having society welcome them back. In fact, soldiers who need debriefing and/or counselling in any way, shape, or form are the weakest of all. Society has such a double standard – this is what we expect of you, but don't you dare ask any of us to measure up to our own standard of acceptability. Fortunately, society does have *some* accepted tools available to make the transition back to society a little more doable. Gary, I am one of those 'accepted' tools. Let me help you through this, just talk to me."

Hearing such politically incorrect truth actually made me think that Brooks was on my side. It made me believe, for the first time, that Brooks genuinely wanted to help me. I asked him where we had bookmarked the end of our previous session. "Where did we leave off last?"

Brooks referred to his notes and reminded me. "I believe you had just blown up the enemy's communications camp."

"Oh, yeah! Right! Going forward from this point is when everything goes downhill."

"The four of us were running back to the lead car but we got cut off by enemy forces. Remember when I told you my misgivings about the repercussions of blowing up the communications camp? Well, my misgivings turned into harsh reality! We had a choice to make: either fight what was in front of us or run into the bigger fight 300 feet behind us. We chose to fight what was in front of us. Oh, what I wouldn't have done to have Handmaiden and her team with us right then. Handmaiden and her team have combat experience that the four of us could not amount to. Their combat experience would even the odds a little because we realized very shortly that the weapons the enemy had were technologically superior to what we had."

We fought handicapped like this for what seemed to be hours. We were losing ground fast. We realized that a miracle had to happen, or we were not going to walk away from this battle! The enemy realized that victory was almost assuredly theirs, and they pressed their attack even harder. Then the miracle happened!

Handmaiden and her team came out of nowhere and attacked them from every direction. Handmaiden and her team fought with such surgical precision, the enemy was completely overwhelmed. Everywhere the enemy turned to run, they were attacked. I had never seen such organized coordination on the battlefield! My esteem for Handmaiden's skill exploded, and I could hardly contain my admiration.

With our enemy routed, I looked up and saw Handmaiden. I started making my way to her with a smile of gratitude on my face. I saw Handmaiden shoot a hard, cold glare my way. Her glare didn't surprise me at all, due to how we performed our mission. Her voice matched her glare. "Do you think this is a joke, Foltz? According to plan, you were supposed to be in and out *fast and quick,* with only hardware damage." With controlled anger, Handmaiden continued. "But no, you had to have drama and blow the place sky high! Every EPC unit in a ten-mile radius is closing in on the AO right now. Now we have to go and help them!"

"Why can't we just go back?" I asked. Just going back seemed like a reasonable solution to me.

Handmaiden could hardly contain her anger. "We can't go back, Folz! The Major has ordered us to go and help our main force at the enemy's base camp!"

I objected to the Major's new orders. "But our orders were to get in and get out and let the main force take the enemies defences."

Handmaiden sternly clarified, "Those *were* our orders until the Major heard about your little stunt, which quickly changed his mind, and not in a good way. The Major does *not* like having his explicit orders ignored. He now has a mess on his hands because of you clowns. He decided to use his one dependable tool at his disposal to clean this up, that one tool being my team. Now let's go before we can no longer get to the main force. We need to get to them before they get cut off."

In my mind, I was taking exception to what I had just been told. The Major thought that blowing the communications tent was my idea? Nothing could be further from the truth. While it was true that Andrews did not have to work too hard to get me to agree with his plan, it was still *his* plan! Andrews knew me well enough to know that my testosterone would start flowing quite easily if he questioned taking direction from a woman! I should have realized that I was being manipulated. But, in the heat of the battle, how do you think through being manipulated? Then, in complete embarrassment, I realized that Handmaiden had been able to do what I had found impossible to do – think. I hated realizing that Andrews had manipulated me. I hated the realization that Handmaiden had shown, in spades, that she was clearly my superior in keeping her head level and her thinking clear. The only thing for me to do was to discipline myself. I had to discipline myself to become a better soldier. I wanted, no, I *needed* to become a better soldier by forcing myself to think clearly despite what was happening around me. People's lives depended on me forcing myself to be better!

"We ran for what felt like hours getting to the battle at the enemy's base camp. My legs were numb. My lungs felt bloated. My body's energy was spent. I was falling behind the group. I forced myself to keep going because I was confident that I could make a difference when we got to the battlefield. I would just need to catch my breath."

Brooks was intrigued by my assertion, so he asked, "What made you so sure you could make a difference, Gary?"

I knew Brooks asked this because there would be lots of people fighting. In order for one person to make a difference, that one person would have to bring a unique skillset. Knowing that Handmaiden was also there, thinking that I had a unique skillset was possibly an overstatement. But I truly thought my experience in Princeton did give me something unique.

"Princeton! My experience in Princeton is the reason why I believed I would make a difference," I answered with genuine assertion.

Brooks was taken a little by surprise with my confidence. "You believed your experience in Princeton would be able to turn the tide of battle?"

"Yes!" I clearly remembered the conviction I had that my experience in Princeton really would make me a difference-maker.

"And how did that work out? Did your Princeton experience make you that difference-maker?" I got the idea that Brooks was truly hoping that I was. I think he wanted his authorized battle notes to be wrong.

With tears and discomfort, I had no choice but to acknowledge the truth. "We fought. We fought with all the fight we had in us. We tried to employ micro strategies, but…" I stopped talking because the truth was very emotionally painful to deal with.

"But what, Gary?!" Brooks yelled angrily. Brooks knew he was having success in getting me debriefed on a situation that I clearly did not want to talk about. He did not want to give me an opportunity to stop talking. Brooks knew we were on the threshold of a breakthrough that I needed but did not want to go through.

My emotions were starting to get the better of me. My eyes were welling up, and tears started to flood my eyes. I blurted out, "There were just too many of them!"

"Because of the location of the enemy's base inside their camp, my team and I were already well inside their camp when we approached from the east side of the enemy's base. Looking back, I now realize that what the enemy was bringing our way made Princeton feel like a massage. It was actually a good thing that we did not know what was coming, otherwise we would probably have surrendered!"

"'Fernsby, get on the horn. Tell Command we are on the offensive heading northwest,'" ordered Andrews.

"Just when Fernsby starting working the radio, we realized what was happening. The enemy had set a trap. We had fallen into their trap face first. The enemy's strategy had worked almost too well! We tried to retreat but got cut off, then we got cornered in what seemed to be a townhouse. Moving from our current position meant certain, immediate, death. We were stuck, nowhere to go, so we did what we were known for... holding the line.

"Our best hope was that reinforcements would come to our aid. The closest thing we got to reinforcements was a helicopter that crashed onto the enemy position. We eventually had no choice but to surrender when we ran out of ammo. Captured by the EPC forces with great ease, it seemed, but we knew whatever was coming wasn't going to be sunshine and rainbows.

"After the helicopter crashed, weren't there any reinforcements? Command wouldn't just leave you out to dry, would they?" asked Dr. Brooks.

"They tried to, but once the EPC surrounded the first wave there was no way to get to us. Outmanned, outmatched and overpowered – it was a classic encirclement," I said resignedly.

"So you got captured by the enemy. What happened next?"

I continued. "They blindfolded us and took us to their field base farther north. About a few hundred miles back from the frontline. We were all put in the same holding cell. Well, I would say calling it a cell is a bit of a stretch. It was a straight-up horse stable.

"Anyways the 'cell' we were put in was very small, and there were about seventy prisoners, give or take, stuck shoulder to shoulder. The prisoners weren't just POWs. They also included civilians, refugees, and 'others.' Some of the 'others' were people claiming to be defectors from places like China, Korea, and Russia."

"One person said he abandoned his post in Belarus on the European front. His name was Maxim."

"'So, Maxim, what was it like on the European front?' I asked.

"'Well, I was conscripted when I was eighteen in 2040. I was on the border of Belarus for about twelve years. I was a rifleman in a division of about fifteen thousand. I was a gunner on one of the invasion vehicles. We called them 'crocs' for their ability to cross no man's land without any real resistance from the terrain.'

"'The crocs had three main compartments in them. At the front was the driver's seat. The driver's seat held three men. In the back was a troop transport. The troop transport fit about fifteen men. Then, on top, was a small compartment that fit one man – the gunner. That man on top – the gunner - had two jobs. His first job was to cover the men exiting the vehicle. His other job was to protect the vehicle when the men were doing a drop-off. My boss assigned me that job on day one.'

Dr. Brooks was interested in what was involved in a 'drop-off.' "How successful was Maxim's first drop-off?"

I answered, "Maxim told me the first smack was doing fine, when he dropped them off. Then Maxim and his company left to continue their 'rounds.' When they returned, Maxim said he saw a trail of pieces of human flesh that stretched for about twenty metres."

Dr. Brooks now had more terms to learn. "What was it that Maxim called a smack?"

I slipped into teaching mode, using Maxim's explanations. "Well, a smack is a group of jellyfish. A jellyfish, or jelly for short, is an individual soldier. They called them this because they got ripped apart easily, like a jellyfish."

"How many of these 'smacks' did Maxim deliver?" Dr. Brooks could not imagine how it must have felt to deliver soldiers directly to their graves. But, in wartime, terrible things happen.

Very solemnly, I answered, "Maxim told me he delivered 422 smacks. He regretted every single man and woman he took to no man's land. Little wonder why Maxim abandoned his post! After Maxim told me that, he was taken away for interrogation. I never saw him again," I said dejectedly.

⌐ CHAPTER 6 ¬
The Walk with a Minotaur

"SO, THE MAN GOT taken away for interrogation. Granted, you did not see him again, but you really don't have any evidence that shows what happened to him. From your perspective, what happened next?" asked Dr. Brooks.

"Well, you are correct. I don't have any clue what happened to him. There were rumours that claimed that our captors' interrogations were unsuccessful. But they could not let those rumours be proven true. If they were, other prisoners would think there is no penalty for being ignorant and not answer their questions.

"Making the prisoner disappear would induce mental torture on the other prisoners, simply because of questions left unanswered. If memory serves me correctly, there were three prevailing rumours about what happened to prisoners who disappeared: they killed him slowly, they sent him to a camp in Siberia, or they sent him to the front lines.

"But if they killed him slowly, they would have put him on display for the rest of us as a message. I doubt this to be true, because killing him slowly would only have affected him. The EPC had already isolated him, so the torture he would have endured would have had no effect on the other prisoners. The rest of us never did see any evidence to support this rumour. Because of this, we thought the other rumours to be more plausible.

"They sent him to a camp in Siberia. This rumour is more plausible than the previous. Part of this rumour claims that he is still there to this day.

"Being held captive in Siberia?! I have heard that there are towns in Siberia that hold world cold-weather records. I have also heard of people and animals being bitten to death by hordes of relentless biting insects in the summer.

"The EPC is not stupid! The EPC's number-one strategy is to work the prisoners to death as quickly as possible while still following internationally accepted prisoner-treatment agreements as closely as they can. The sooner the prisoner succumbs to their living conditions, the sooner prisoner transfers can be managed. Just thinking about the hell those prisoners live through makes me squirm!

"They could have also sent him to the Canadian front lines. This rumour has a viable explanation. There are parts of Canada where the living conditions mirror those of Siberia! Knowing the EPC's objective to keep prisoner transfers happening, you can bet they will send the prisoner to the harshest living conditions they can find. Like I said, these are just rumours. Because of the nature of the rumours, I think that our captors instigated them," I replied.

Dr. Brooks had a strange look on his face, but he quickly explained, "I meant what happened next for you."

"Oh." I was a little annoyed. For me to answer his question the way he wanted, he should have qualified his question – him being a doctor and all! I really did think he should have been able to figure that out before I gave him my long-winded answer.

I continued, "Well, our captors continued to keep us in the stable for a few more days. Some of us were sporadically taken out for questioning. I would imagine that the costs of keeping a relatively small number of prisoners at our location were beginning to add up. Soon the EPC command decided to take us out of the country. The command sent us to a prison in what seemed to be Eastern Asia."

I could see that Dr. Brooks looked confused. He asked, "How could you tell where you were? My report says that you were shipped over in sea cans with no windows or ability to see outside."

I explained, "One of the prisoners told me. When we got there, the weather indicated we were in either northern China, eastern Mongolia, or southern Russia."

"Was he correct?" Dr. Brooks questioned.

"Actually, yeah. We soon found out that we were in an improvised POW camp in eastern Mongolia," I answered.

I continued, "Finding out that we were in eastern Mongolia confirmed to me what I had previously suspected about the rumours we had heard. The EPC wanted our brains to imagine horrific destinations where they had sent missing prisoners!!"

Dr. Brooks, now intrigued about this POW camp, asked, "Please describe what it was like in this new camp."

I answered, "I was there for five years. Every day I was there was absolute boredom. I did the same thing every day for those five years. The mental fatigue we endured was numbing. We had nothing to read. We were not allowed anything to write with. There was always an EPC guard within earshot, so even our conversations were monitored. Some of the others became so paranoid they became suspicious of their own shadows. Some of them went so far as to report to their guards when they became convinced that their shadows had moved!"

"What did you do for five years, Gary?" Dr. Brooks asked.

I answered, "I did the only thing I was allowed to do to maintain any semblance of sanity. The only thing I was allowed to do was to build and repair machines."

Dr. Brooks had a very puzzled look on his face. "Come on, Gary, do you really expect me to believe that the EPC would allow a prisoner to build and repair machines? I mean, how would they benefit from your building and repairing machines?"

I explained, "Well, there is no doubt that I had to disguise mind-challenging activities as something that would directly benefit them. I also knew that I would have to do my best to oversell the direct benefit to them. I racked my brain over this for a couple of weeks. How did I get the EPC to condone me working on a seemingly harmless project that they would consider beneath them to pay attention to??

"One day, I heard a commotion by a rundown shack not far from my tent. I heard two or three EPC soldiers seemingly swearing at something. I took a closer look at what they were attempting to do.

"They were trying to unload a medium-sized window air conditioner from a flatbed truck. One of the soldiers saw me and immediately told his compatriots that they should force me to 'finish the job.' They surrounded me, so I had little choice but to use my high school physics. Fortunately, there was a sizeable ledge around the perimeter of the flat bed. I found two 4"x 4" posts on the flatbed. The posts were about six feet long. I leaned the posts against the flatbed perimeter nearest to the air conditioner. I got up on the flatbed and slid the air conditioner as close to the edge as I dared, right next to the posts. I jumped back down to the ground and placed good-sized rocks at the base of the posts. I gave both of the rocks a good kick to plant them into the soft soil and grass. I walked between the posts to the side of the flat bed and put my hands on the sides of the air conditioner. The EPC guards were watching me very closely. In my head I knew I had to make this look good.

"The truth is that I really did not know how easy it would be to slide the air conditioner down the ramp. I had no clue if the air conditioner would slide. Yes, I had purposely looked for posts that were longer to avoid dealing with a lot of weight. My life might very well depend on success. I did know that the air conditioner seemed to slide on the flat bed with comparable ease, but I did not know why it slid with ease! Had someone spilled grease or oil on the flatbed?? I took a quick look and my brief observation seemed to discount that possibility.

"I braced myself as best I could. Would I be nominated for an Oscar award for my acting, or would there actually be no acting? I took another look at the head soldier, who was watching me intently. I grabbed the sides of the air conditioner and tilted it ever so carefully toward me. Almost as if on cue, the air conditioner slid off of the flat bed and onto the 4"x4"s and stuck. I was as shocked as anyone would have been! I shuffled my feet back a few inches, keeping my body braced and not moving my hands.

"I relieved the upward pressure just the smallest bit, and the air conditioner slid down the posts just the smallest bit. I repeated that procedure until the air conditioner was on the ground. Just for good measure, I added a few well-placed, but very much unneeded, grunts and groans. I also feigned the need for a rest by collapsing beside the air conditioner. The fact that I was now covered in sweat seemed to sell the whole act.

"The lead soldier pointed to the man-door on the shed and motioned me there. I put the two posts side by side and slid the air conditioner along them until it was inside the door. I feigned the need for additional rest to give me a minute to see what was in the shed.

"After a few seconds, my eyes adjusted to the dim light. There were all kinds of small machines in the shed. Some of the machines looked like they just needed a new switch, while others looked like they needed more attention. As far as the EPC soldiers were concerned, none of the machines worked. The shed was simply the machines' graveyard!

This shed could be a gold mine for me. I had to remind myself to act like working on those machines was the last thing I wanted to do.

"The lead soldier told me to stay where I was, just inside the graveyard. He disappeared for a few minutes and then returned. He told me, in his badly broken English, that he had told his boss about the air conditioner. He told me that his boss reasoned that if I could get the air conditioner off the truck, I should be able to fix some of the machines in the graveyard.

"I never did figure that logic out! I mean, how does physics translate into small-machine repair? Then I remembered that I really don't care how the translation happened. The one person in the camp who could help me escape the mind-numbing monotony of the camp was giving me an opportunity.

"The psychological game was on! The lead's boss and I were going to go head to head! My biggest challenge now was to convince the lead's boss that I did not want to accept the offer to repair those machines. But I had tempered my objections so that the boss would be pleased to insist on making me do something that he wanted done but he was sure that I didn't want to do.

"I decided to simply stand resolutely at ease and focus my eyes on nothing. After only a few seconds of that, I felt a very hard blow to the back of my head. I crumpled to the floor. The boss yelled something at his lead. The lead kicked the side of my rib cage and barked at me, 'Boss says fix machines or you get 'the pit'!' I did not know what 'the pit' was, but I figured that my beating should be enough to sell the boss that I would work on the machines, albeit begrudgingly. I got up off the floor. I checked the back of my head for blood. Thankfully my hand, while it was covered in sweat, held no blood.

"The boss barked something else at his lead. His lead then turned to me with a smirk and told me, 'Whether you want to or not, you are going to help us win the war!' Both he and his boss began to laugh with a crazy laugh. They were clearly pleased with themselves. In their minds, they had devised a way to save the EPC some money on fixing machines. They imagined their higher bosses heaping praise upon them for figuring out how to get the machines fixed and availing more money to supply their front lines with needed equipment."

Dr. Brooks was actually ahead of me in my story. He asked, "If the EPC is so smart, why don't they send broken machines and equipment to your camp and have you fix them? Please go into more detail."

I continued, "What the boss and his lead did not know was that the EPC had a contract with the Hyenas. The contract with the Hyenas gave the EPC forces the technology that the Hyenas had developed in the 2030s.

"When the EPC command found out that our camp was fixing all kinds of machines from our graveyard, they put a partial stop to ordering new machines. Command wanted to find out how successful the machine repairs were. After a couple of weeks without complaints about the repaired machines, EPC command set out to exploit this new resource to the fullest.

"The boss and his lead were not pleased with this development. All the praise that they had imagined coming from EPC command seemingly evaporated before their eyes. They did not realize that their command wanted all that praise for themselves. Seemed logical to me, but to stay alive, I kept my mouth shut! The EPC got everything from war machines to rifles and ammunition. They made me fix minotaurs.

"Minotaurs are war machines that stand about twenty feet tall and weigh over a hundred American tons. The minotaur weight does not include the weapons and ammunition that are designed to attach to the machine. When the second wave of military action happened in '54 in Eastern Europe, I fixed and enhanced the weapons the EPC used.

"I really had my doubts about some of the enhancements that the EPC wanted done to the weapons. The enhancements were similar to trying to put a square peg into a much- smaller round hole. I really had to use brainpower to make them work! Fortunately, the EPC did not care how the enhancement worked; they just wanted it to work. Every once in a while the lead guy would help me to remember that the enhancement(s) had to work flawlessly. But that was exactly why I had done the role-playing to get this gig. I was very thankful that I had had a father who was an exceptional problem solver and took great pride in imparting that gift to his son.

"Other countries also had clear waves of military action, like northern Australia from early April to late May 2054. Also, Egypt had some short-lived action in April of 2054. Turkey probably had one of the longest stretches of fighting, from September 2054 to early January 2055.

"My efforts kept me alive and my mind fully occupied. Unfortunately, my efforts were also crucial in helping my enemy kill the soldiers of my country's allies. I had to work hard at concentrating on staying alive.

"Did you know that the Minotaur has a heavy-duty combat camera above the cockpit? I came to despise those cameras! I had to watch the tapes of my allies dying every day for five years. Initially, I blamed myself for the deaths of our allies.

Then I realized that, sooner or later, the EPC would have found someone else to do what I was doing. I reasoned that if I had wanted this fixing gig in order to help the EPC kill the allies, then yes, I would have been responsible. The fact was that I had taken this gig merely for survival. Yes, it was very unfortunate how my efforts were being bastardized, but I had no control over that. I was doing my gig to stay alive, pure and simple. My initial purpose in this gig was to fix air conditioners and photocopiers. I had no way of knowing about the Hyenas contract."

Dr. Brooks, full of questions and confusion, asked, "Why did you have to watch the tapes?"

I answered solemnly, "The EPC made us watch the footage to brainwash us. The EPC wanted us to believe that they were mercilessly overpowering the allies everywhere, and we were losing... badly."

"Did this type of torture work on you and your fellow POWs?" Dr. Brooks questioned.

I continued, "It worked on some of us. Remember when I told you about prisoners reporting that their shadows had moved? Well, I firmly believe that they saw their shadows move because the mental torture was quite effective, and they had given up hope. Other prisoners, like myself, recognized the footage for what it was and ignored it. Our objective was on trying to survive one day at a time."

Dr. Brooks wanted more information on the Minotaur cockpit camera footage. "Explain what you saw on the footage they showed you."

"What I saw was a bloodbath. Our forces in Europe were not prepared, or equipped, to handle the weapons the Hyenas gave to the EPC. The Minotaur enabled the EPC to move faster, hit harder, and shoot more accurately.

"All the work the EU had done to hold the eastern front for twenty-four years was destroyed in the last four years. There had been over 3 million men and women holding that defensive front. The EPC managed to slaughter about seventy-five percent of that force in those last four years! Thank goodness my brother Ethan survived. He was very lucky."

Dr. Brooks, curious about my brother, asked, "Did your brother tell you about his experience in the field?"

"If you are asking if my brother told me about how hard it was to fight when outmanned and outgunned, then yes!"

"Are you comfortable with telling me what he told you?" Dr. Brooks asked empathetically.

I did not bother answering Brooks's question. Rather, I just continued with the story, "My brother told me the fifties were the hardest of all the years he was there."

Dr. Brooks was clearly intrigued, and asked, "Why were the fifties the hardest of all the years he was there?"

I explained, "Because that was the decade when the EPC were getting warfare technology from the Hyenas. Remember that Minotaur war machine? It was designed to rip through the latest tank models like a hot knife through butter. My brother's battle company called them tank shredders because of how quickly a Minotaur could destroy a tank."

"How did your brother survive?" asked Dr. Brooks.

"He barely survived!" I clarified. "My brother was the sole survivor from his whole battle company of fourteen tanks and dozens of crewmen. To this day, he has no idea how he survived."

Dr. Brooks, impressed with my progress in being able to talk about all kinds of events, ended the session. "Well, Gary, you have made lots of progress over the amount of time we have had. How does next week, Sunday at ten a.m., sound to you?"

"That sounds good to me, doc. I will see you then," I replied and left.

For whatever reason, I felt relief. Dr. Brooks could probably explain it, him being a doctor and all. All I knew is that I felt a small victory over some of the demons I had been wrestling with.

I arrived late at my dad's place again, but something was wrong. Dad was lying on the floor with a big bottle of dark rum beside him. There were also probably two dozen crushed cans of what looked like light beer scattered about.

I picked Dad up, brought him to his room, and put him to bed. When Dad was safely in bed, the realization that the war affected him harder than anyone else in the family really hit me.

Dad was stuck making machines in a factory, hoping not to receive bad news from the government. Dad's warfare was the ultimate mental battle of everyone from his life disappearing like sugar in the rain. There was absolutely nothing he could do to change the outcome. My battle in Princeton was a physical battle. In a physical battle, your brain can devote all its time and energy to survival.

For whatever reason, I began rummaging through Dad's things. I found his 2018 high school yearbook. He had graduated high school in 2018. I flipped through the pages, looking to find his picture from forty-five years ago. Even before I found it, I found pages of graduates whose faces had been crossed out in red. I had a very good idea why these peoples' faces had been crossed out, but I wanted to be sure. I went to Dad's computer. I wanted to search the list of those known to have died in the war.

I looked at one of the crossed-out faces. Her name was 'Molly Adams.' I typed her name in the search bar. Her picture and information appeared on the monitor. Molly had died thirty years ago, in Australia, from radiation poisoning. She was unlucky enough to live through a nuclear explosion. Instead, Molly languished in agonizing pain as the radiation dissolved her body from the inside. She died hours later.

I flipped hastily through a few more pages. I found another picture with a crossed-out face. The face belonged to 'Kris Edson.' Kris had died in the Kocatepe bombings in 2030. He had gone for a walk outside the local mosque when a bomb exploded. Kris died instantly from the blast.

I continued flipping through the yearbook for about another hour. Everyone he had crossed out was either dead or assumed dead because they went MIA. He had been crossing out their faces for the last thirty years.

Then I found my mother's picture. Her face was crossed out. Finding my mother confused me because my dad told me that he met Mom in college. I typed her name, 'Eleanor Foltz,' in the search bar. She died on January 4, 2033, in a field hospital in Ukraine. The hospital had been bombed during an artillery strike. The medic said she died instantly.

My father had never told me how she died. When I asked him about it, all he said was, "She didn't deserve to die like that." Now that I knew how she died, I was both relieved and perplexed. I was relieved that Mom had not suffered the same fate as Molly. I was perplexed because Dad made it sound like he would rather have had Mom linger in agony, and that did not sound like the loving husband I knew Dad was to her.

I did a head count on how many graduates there were in his graduating class. There were roughly 950, and of them, there were only 38 still assumed to be alive. These numbers represented about 910 people wanting to make their mark on the world; 910 people wanting to get good jobs, find "the" one, settle down, and enjoy what life has to offer.

Then the war happens and steals from them what life had to offer.

This war really did take everything away from my dad. I wondered how many of my classmates from 2044 were still alive. Finding this yearbook really put the war into perspective for me. I looked at the list on the computer again. I wanted to look at the total losses for both sides. Since the bombings in 2030, the total losses so far were 994,834,642. This war had taken the lives of almost one billion people.

Most people cannot identify with a number like one billion. I disciplined myself to think in terms of one million. Well, one BILLION is the same as one million people dying every day for almost three years. How do people truly wrap their heads around numbers like that?!

I have seen what one man can do to another man. What one man can do to another man is bad enough! The world is now finding out what one powerful man can do to many men. The mayhem that that one powerful man can inflict is sickening. I guess my father and I were the lucky ones and the unlucky ones.

⌐ CHAPTER 7 ¬
Outburst

"SO, GARY, HOW DID this past week go for you?" asked Dr. Brooks.

I really didn't care much for Brooks's question. It insinuated that he was trying to be subtle while hoping that I would volunteer what he was really hoping to hear. The only loophole I could afford Dr. Brooks was that the effects of what I talked about in our last meeting could have had the potential of messing with my brain. If Brooks was concerned that what we talked about would mess with my brain, I would have had more respect for him if he just asked that instead of trying, unsuccessfully, to be subtle.

"I was arrested on Friday. The cops took me to the police station for attacking someone," I said with some confusion. I was confused because I did not know how Brooks would have known about the arrest. I mean, why else would he start the session differently than any of our other sessions?

Dr. Brooks opened his notebook and started writing. After a minute, he asked me, "Can you explain why you attacked this person, Gary?"

Obviously, the fact that I mentioned my arrest was exactly what Brooks wanted to hear. Even more confused than before, I answered him. "No, I can't explain why I attacked. I don't know what provoked my aggression. It all happened so fast and so unexpectedly, I did not have time to control myself."

Dr. Brooks, very intrigued by both what happened and my inability to explain why it happened, asked, "Just start from the beginning, Gary. Tell me everything you can remember about how you first encountered the situation. Then, mentally work your way to the attack."

"Well, my dad and I were out of milk, so I walked to the grocery store to get some. When I got there, I started browsing the dairy products. From behind me, I felt somebody's hand on my shoulder. Instinctively, my combat training took over my decision-making. As far as I was concerned, this person was my enemy, and I had to defend myself. I grabbed this person's hand, hoisted them over my shoulder, and slammed them into the ground. As quick as lightning, my other hand clamped around the enemy's throat, attempting to choke them into submission. Why anyone would choose physical contact, from behind, over a vocal greeting to get my attention is beyond me. That's what people do in horror movies, and it never goes well!"

Dr. Brooks, very absorbed in my story, asked, "And you remember all of this?"

I knew that Brooks' question was another way of asking for more details, so I obliged. "No. I don't remember any of it. What I told you is what the police told me. The last thing I actually remember is that I was looking at the milk and deciding which type to get. I momentarily blacked out. My body just naturally reacted to the situation and took it to the extreme. My brain kicked back on and I saw this woman struggling on the ground in front of me. She had my hand wrapped around her throat. I immediately let her go, stood up, and ran out of the store. I ran straight back home in a state of panic."

"When you got called into the station, what happened there?" Dr. Brooks asked.

I answered him with solemn contempt. "They told me she was trying to get my attention so she could talk to me about my scars. Apparently she wanted to ask about them because she is a novelist writing about World War 3 veterans in Canada. She is used to having her tactics questioned, but she maintains there are a lot fewer World War 3 veterans in Canada than one would think. People are always challenging her on her assertion of fewer Canadian vets, so she did her homework. Her results revealed that Canada pulled out of the war seven months ago because of heavy casualties. Canada had experienced unusually high incidents of personnel killed in action as a direct result of being wounded in action. Long story short, some of the wounded were getting forced into battle.

"I still do not understand why she would ignore the fact that I had undergone combat training. She knows what war does to a person. She must have known that the safest thing for her to do was to just wait until she could get in front of me. She must have known that if I did not respond to her voice that I would have been deep in thought. She must have known that to disturb a person who has had combat training is dangerous when they are deep in thought."

Dr. Brooks was in wonder of the number of vets, and he asked, "When you say there are fewer Canadian World War 3 veterans than one would think, how many are there?"

"Well, after the Northwestern European front got hammered from late 2061 to mid-2062…" After I said 2062, I realized I needed a minute. "Hold on a minute. I have to think the numbers through." I take a long pause, trying to remember how many of us got out. I continued. "There were roughly eight thousand of us after we got steamrolled by the EPC. The prime minister ordered all of us to pull out of Europe. The prime minister added a short but stern piece of advice: 'If you want to stay, Canada will not be able to help you until after the end of the war.'"

"How many of the eight thousand stayed?" questioned Dr. Brooks.

I replied, "Roughly six thousand of the eight thousand stayed in Europe to fight, the other two thousand went home."

"Alright. Your observation of the situation is quite objective and fair." Dr. Brooks inquired further, "And of the two thousand that came home, how many of them are still alive?"

I answered, "The last time I checked, we numbered barely in the hundreds."

Dr. Brooks looks down at his notes again and said something that caught me off guard. "Let me ask this: Of the two thousand evacuated, how many either couldn't deal with the PTSD and committed suicide, died of wounds and sickness, or disappeared from society?"

I was surprised that his analysis of what happened to these people mirrored mine. I remarked, "You literally took the words out of my mouth! How do you know these facts?"

Dr. Brooks, amused, and pleased, with my observation, replied, "I researched about Canadian war vets. Let's just say that my research did not leave me with much personal time this past week."

"Well, the time you used for your research definitely paid off. Those facts are the exact... truth!" I said with slight surprise. I wasn't expecting him to be this devoted to his patients, especially when he has over a hundred and fifty.

Dr. Brooks responded, "Well, I am very devoted to my patients. Without my patients, I would be nothing." With a smirk, he added, "In all likelihood, I would probably be working in a soup kitchen in Europe." He continued, "I do have to say that some of my patients are more interesting than others. With no compliment intended, you are one of my more interesting cases. Anyways..." Dr. Brooks wanted to get back on track. "We were talking about why the journalist wanted to talk but you ended up throwing her over your shoulder like a sack of potatoes, correct?"

"Correct," I replied a little sheepishly. I really did not like the analogy, but I couldn't fault him because his description fit quite accurately.

"Have you talked with her since then to try to apologize?" inquired Dr. Brooks.

"No, I haven't talked with her," I replied with chagrin. "Talking with someone who is avoiding you is difficult to do!" Right after I said that I realized how pathetic it sounded. When a man wants to talk with a person, he figures out a way to make it happen. No amount of avoidance from the other person is going to stop him.

"Ok. What's her name?" asked Dr. Brooks. He sounded like he wanted to help me talk to her without outright calling me out.

I replied, "I think they said her name is Kendall Wilson. I am not too sure." I was pretty sure that Brooks considered my lack of ingenuity in tracking her down to be attributed to my PTSD. Then Brooks verified my suspicion that he wanted to help me get an audience with the journalist. "Well, I will look into it. I will see if I can facilitate you two getting an interview together." Then, with a smirk, he teased, "After the interview, you can just throw her over your shoulder again, okay?"

I was actually quite perturbed with the teasing, and I let him know. "Don't kid about a thing like that! She almost sued me. Getting sued is not something to joke about. Just the thought of being sued scares me half to death!" I was pretty sure Brooks knew he had crossed the line, and I was emphatic to get him back where he belonged!

"Ok, consider the interview scheduled. Sometime in the next few months, I will email you a time and a place." Dr. Brooks continued. "Now let's continue with what you were talking about from our last session. We were talking about repairing Minotaurs, but tell me about the day-to-day life of a POW. Were there prisoners from organizations other than RUD (Republic of United Democracies) in the camp?"

I was actually impressed with Brooks. He had obviously read my reaction quite accurately. Without saying anything about "crossing the line," he certainly implied his apology by getting back to the matter for which I was there.

"You are correct. There were prisoners in the camp who were not from RUD. There were hardened criminals, convicted defectors, and there were also civilians there. It was not a friendly environment," I said.

Brooks wanted to know what happened in the prison that I considered noteworthy. "Tell me some of the things that stood out to you in the prison."

"Well, something that stood out to me was how confident and calm the civilians were. They never disturbed the peace. They never challenged anyone. The civilians stuck together. If anyone challenged them, the guards would intervene. The civilians were, by far, the most intimidating group of people in the prison during my time there," I replied.

"Anything else that stood out to you?" asked Dr. Brooks again. I got the feeling that Brooks wanted me to talk about something specific without giving me any hint of what he was looking for. I guess that meant that my answer would be spontaneous, which really was best.

"The control that the commanding officer had over us. You had to be awake, dressed, and standing at 0700 hours, which means you would have to wake up about ten minutes prior."

"What would happen if someone missed that deadline?" asked Dr. Brooks.

"The guards dragged them out of their cell. We never saw them again," I replied.

Astonished from what I said, Dr. Brooks took a short pause to reply. "Do you know what would happen to them?"

I replied, "There were only rumours. One rumour was that they were exiled to the Gobi Desert. Another rumour was that they were sent to Europe to be worked to death. Personally,

I really don't know what happened to them. I really did not care what happened to them because I was too focussed on my own survival!"

Dr. Brooks looked at some notes he had. He asked me a question referring to something I said a few days prior. "Other than the psychological torture you and your fellow soldiers endured, what else did they do to you?"

"The guards did a lot of things to us. They seemed to enjoy going way overboard in response to a request. For instance, one time a guy got waterboarded for asking for water. Usually, though, they punished you if you weren't working hard enough or if you were moving too slowly," I replied.

"What did they do to you Gary?" asked Dr. Brooks.

"They did nothing to me, Doctor. I was a good prisoner. I was very careful not to rock the boat. I did what I was asked without hesitation," I said nervously.

Dr. Brooks narrowed his eyes and leaned forward almost imperceptibly. With pursed lips, he almost whispered, "I know you are lying to me, Gary."

I purposely put an indignant tone in my voice, and, very defensively, I replied, "I am *not* lying. I am telling you the blatant truth."

Dr. Brooks leaned back in his chair as if he was playing poker and still had an ace up his sleeve. "Ok. If you aren't lying to me, then tell me where you got all of those scars on your body. Please tell me the story behind every single one of those scars." Brooks was so confident that he had me cornered in a lie. He was calling my bluff.

I was getting nervous because Brooks sounded like he had some inside information on me. I was bluffing but I was also angry that Brooks was calling my bluff. I was just not going to give him the satisfaction of knowing that he had gotten under my skin. Very calmly, I fabricated plausible explanations of where all the scars came from, "Ok, all the scars on my hands, back of my skull, shoulder, ribs and wrist are from Princeton. The scars on my arms come from Kabul. My scarred eyebrow is a reminder from a biking accident when I was seven. Are you happy now that I told you where I got every scar on my body?"

With a smirk on his face, Brooks said, "You forgot something, Gary."

"Oh yeah! And what do you think I forgot?" I retorted with reluctant annoyance.

Instead of just answering me, Brooks closed his notebook. He looked like he was ready to put the final nail in the trap I had willingly fallen into, and continued, "Let me tell you a story from a former prisoner at the same prison you went to, Gary. He told me about how they punished you if you didn't obey, work fast enough or do a good job. You know what they did, Gary?" asked Dr. Brooks with a slight, pursed smile.

"You tell me, Doc, you seem bent on trapping me in my supposed lie!" I replied with overwhelming anxiety.

"They put shackles on your ankles, which were attached to chains. But what they did next was the painful part. They then attached the chains to two fifty-pound cement blocks, one for each foot. The guards then threw the blocks down into an old, dry water well and filled the well with enough water that the prisoner had to use his arms to swim. The prisoner could not tread water because his feet were attached to the chains. The prisoner would be left there for days, maybe even weeks at a time. If the prisoner survived, the guards branded his right leg in the shape of a sea turtle," said Dr. Brooks

As I crossed my left leg over my right to hide the brand he was talking about, I replied, "That is an interesting story. I will have to tell that to my kids one day."

Dr. Brooks was confused by my response, so he continued to call me out. "I saw the brand on your leg the first day you came in here, Gary. Those scars you said that you got on your hands in Princeton aren't from having your fingers broken or from crawling in rough terrain for two years. Those scars are from steel-studded whip lashes on your hands and forearms." Dr. Brooks was a little more than annoyed with me for trying to hide the truth from him.

I retaliated and blurted out, "Yeah, and how do you know these specific scars on certain people? You were never in the front lines like I was, all you have been doing is hiding behind a desk during this war!"

Dr. Brooks was stunned from my retaliation and replied, "You know what happens to a prisoner that doesn't wake up on time, Gary?"

I replied, "Other than being ripped from his cell and taken away, no. I already told you that nobody knows."

Dr. Brooks sighed, put his right leg on the coffee table, rolled up his pant leg, and said, "Well, Gary, let me tell you. The prisoner gets put into a rail car. He is sent to the deadliest place on Earth at that time. They may make the prisoner clear minefields. If that doesn't kill him, the prisoner becomes a human pack mule, carrying who knows what across the Middle Eastern front. If *that* doesn't kill him, they send him to Africa on a pool noodle, hoping you drown. But if that doesn't kill him, they send the prisoner home where nobody will greet or thank him. Then he becomes a shrink for other army vets from around the world." With as much sarcasm as Brooks could muster, he ended the session with, "Have a good day, Gary. I will see you next week. You can call to set up the day and time!"

⌜ CHAPTER 8 ⌝
A Ghost in the Wild

EFT WITH NOTHING, NOT even an emotion. Left with no intent to return, stormed out with a fury of anger but mass confusion; I was scared that he would try to run back to the spearhead that he came from, always running from something or someone. Then I remembered that I myself couldn't even grasp the idea of holding back the force of a hammer with a toothpick. When I fought, it was hammer to hammer, iron to iron, fist to fist, man… to man.

I fought on the frontline with millions, against millions. He fought on the bullseye surrounded by darts. Still, we had our comparisons.

Both incarcerated against our will, trapped in an unknown land trying to hold back the ocean. I was a rodent surrounded by prey, he was a wounded predator in the same place as me, same place… but not quite the same time. After I got tossed around in the hands of evil, I heard about this wounded predator, I heard his story, after his captors moved him over to the land of spirituality. His captors couldn't hold him back as he escaped his captivity and tore his way through the lands all the way back to his den of a home.

I understood this creature's struggle but I didn't; it was the same story but a different animal, a different perspective, a different body, a different mind... a different soul.

This beast of a creature excelled in every way possible known and unknown to man. Even against the highest of highest odds, he continued to live life to the fullest, and kept doing great things even after he spent himself of resources mentally and physically.

Nobody knows of him, but he has done things beyond description. He hasn't won a Nobel Prize, but he has been to hell and back. He hasn't been inducted into the hall of fame, but fame is an understatement for someone like this. All this person was and had been was a ghost... a Ghost in the Wild.

⌐ CHAPTER 9 ¬
Elephant in the Room

A FTER DR. BROOKS'S OUTBURST at the end of our last session, I anticipated tension between him and me to start this session. In an effort to ease the tension between us, and to try to calm myself, I had brought a couple olive branches. My olive branches were a pack of doughnuts and a story unrelated to the war. I had remembered it quite unexpectedly, and it was one that I could tell Dr. Brooks.

Depending on Dr. Brooks's mood, the doughnuts and story could be viewed as either a feeble attempt at an apology, or as a gallant attempt to take responsibility for a situation that I had created from my refusal to acknowledge the truth. I could only hope Dr. Brooks would receive them as the latter.

When I arrived in the waiting room, I waited for the usual ten to twenty minutes. Today was different. Today was different because the mood in the room was different. The room had a grim feeling to it. The other patients looked at me like they knew what had happened between Dr. Brooks and me last week. I didn't even feel safe being here. I got slightly paranoid and suspected that everyone in the room, besides the staff, were ex-military of some kind. I think one of the guys was part of the Dragon Skin program. Was that thought ever a blast from the past! I had a very brief flashback to when I was offered a position in the Dragon Skin program about ten years ago.

Nevertheless, I was scared just to be in that room. I wanted to get out of there. My whole body was screaming to either get in Dr. Brooks's office or just leave all together.

A man sitting relatively close beside me leaned over and asked with a smirk, "When are you going to start sharing those doughnuts with us?"

His question caught me completely off guard. I had been so involved in my own thoughts that snapping back to reality actually confused me. I turned to him with a very blank expression, still trying to focus on the present. I wanted to be sure of what he had said, so I asked, "Excuse me, what did you say?"

The man, keeping that smirk on his face, replied, "Are we all going to share the doughnuts you have there, or do we have to beg for them?"

I was now confused because the scariest-looking man I had seen since I got back was asking me for a doughnut. Somehow, my brain just could not process that irony. Instead of trying to make sense of it, I simply passed the box of doughnuts around, which gave me time to process that a man's appearance had no connection to the doughnuts, other than mere coincidence.

The doughnut box being passed around seemed to have somewhat of a magical effect on the mood in the room. I could see that everyone, including myself, was less on edge. When the box got back to me, one by one, we started to share stories about ourselves. We were no longer total strangers. Knowing something about each other enabled a bond of brotherhood among us to form, at least temporarily. I did not know how long that bond would last. I really didn't care. I no longer felt afraid to be in the same room as these men, and I had a scary-looking man and a box of doughnuts to thank for that!

One man told us of the time he had played soccer with the EPC soldiers because both sides had run out of ammo and fuel. "It was fun playing soccer then and there. Even though every man was exhausted from the fighting, somehow we all found new energy for fun! Playing soccer at such a ridiculous time and venue helped me remember to enjoy the little things."

Another man told us about the time he picked up a lemur in the Philippines. He had decided to make the lemur a pet and named him Randy. With a sad smile on his face, he lamented a little, saying, "Randy really helped me get through the fighting in the Pacific. To be honest, it was horrific, but Randy's complete innocence helped me remember that not everything had an ulterior motive."

The man beside me told us how he met his wife in Europe. "After we held back one of the drone attacks, I came back with cuts on my face and neck. My CO sent me to the medical tent. An absolute angel of a woman treated me. I tried, quite unsuccessfully, to get her face out of my head. I had heard stories of guys who had fallen for a pretty face only to find out she was with someone else or not interested, and I didn't want that to happen to me.

"One day I swallowed hard and asked Sarah if I could talk to her for a minute. To my absolute surprise and shock, her face lit up like a Christmas tree with the most beautiful smile. When she spoke, she had the most beautifully feminine voice I had ever heard. She answered, 'Sir, you have been an absolute gentleman. You have always treated me with the utmost kindness and respect. I have watched you in your interaction with other women because I wanted to know if you were just putting on a show for me. I am pretty sure that your mother was, or is, a very wise woman. She wanted to be sure her son was raised to treat women the way they deserve to be treated. However, I do have to say that I have noticed that there is something different in your dealings with me as opposed to your dealings with other women. I want to be very honest with you, sir. I have had many suitors. At first, I was quite flattered when I thought that men wanted my company. Unfortunately, I found out rather quickly the men did not necessarily want my *company*. I became quite incensed with the lies that men would tell me just to put another notch in their belts.

'Fortunately for me, I have a mother who was wise enough to teach me, from a very early age, what the majority of men want. Of course, I did not believe her. I wanted men to want the house, kids, and that white picket fence. I held on to that want for a long time.

Shortly after leaving home, I realized that I had to do my own homework on a man. Eventually I was forced to let go of wanting a man to want what I longed for. That does NOT mean that I lowered my standards. It does mean that I simply had to do my own homework on a man if he should happen to get my attention.

'Let me tell you that a woman doing her homework on a man in a man's world, without anyone catching on, is difficult! Sir, I tell you all of that to give you some background of the implications of what I am about to say: I am not married, and I do not have a boyfriend.'

"After Sarah told me that, I did everything in my power to spend as much time with her as possible. Time spent with her just felt natural. I was greatly relieved by Sarah's brutal and blunt honesty. Her honesty enabled me to be me, and when we did things together, we had fun. We laughed a lot. Usually we laughed together at silly things. When we laughed together, we realized we had a shared sense of humour. I also found out that she could tell a story about anything and make me laugh. When Canada pulled out of the war, we settled down and started a family."

These men had great stories. I wish I could have stayed to hear them all, but Dr. Brooks called me shortly after the man beside me ended his story.

Now I had to tell Dr. Brooks my story from where we left off last week. Dr. Brooks, being a very straightforward man, told me, "About last week, Gary, I must apologize about my behaviour. I overreacted and should not have raised my voice. I also yelled at you. I am sorry. Raising my voice and yelling at you are both unprofessional. Before we begin, is there anything you want to say to me?"

I sat there in slight awe and wonder. I understood where Brooks was coming from. I knew we were good to continue from where we left off, after I apologized. I answered, "I am sorry, too, Doc. I had no idea of what you had been through. You have my deepest apologies."

Dr. Brooks replied, "Is that everything?"

After a very brief pause to make sure there was nothing else on my mind, I answered, "Yes. Yes, I believe that covers everything."

Dr. Brooks, slightly relieved, said, "Good. Now we can continue from where we left off. You were telling me about your time in the prison in Mongolia."

I realized I would need Brooks to give me a benchmark at which to begin. I asked him, "Where do you want me to begin there?"

Dr. Brooks answered, "Tell me about the end of your time there."

"The end of my time in Mongolia was the hardest part to survive. The end was also the hardest part to forget. Thirty percent of the prisoners died from hunger, disease, and random executions by the guards. Taking care of the corpses was next to impossible because it was wintertime."

Dr. Brooks, interested in my story, asked, "Why was it so hard to take care of the bodies just because it was wintertime, Gary?"

I replied with a slight sadness. "In wintertime, the ground is frozen. We couldn't bury the bodies. We tried burning the bodies, but we could not find wood in the prison camp that was dry enough. Every time we got a small fire started, the frozen moisture in the wood would snuff the fire out before we could burn the bodies."

"So, how did you dispose of the bodies?" asked Dr. Brooks.

I replied, "I knew there were used batteries in the war machine shop where I worked. We took the batteries out of the shop, pried the cell covers off, poured the battery acid into pails, and mixed the acids together. The acid mixture proved quite effective at dissolving the corpses."

Dr. Brooks wanted a little more detail, so he lightly pressed, "Explain to me how the process worked, please."

I took a sip of water and a deep breath and continued. "The pails we were allowed to use for the acid mixture were not big enough for full corpses. I suspected that was done on purpose by the guards for their own safety. We had to cut the bodies up, bring the pieces to the pails, and dump the pieces into the acid pails. Sometimes it would get so cold the acid would freeze with the body parts in the bucket.

"Of all the things I was forced to do in that camp, I most despised having to remove all bodily evidence that these men lived. Soon my loathing for what those guards made us do translated into an absolute passion to escape. I knew I had to be careful because I did not want to be caught and disappear."

Dr. Brooks, intrigued, asked, "How did you get out of the prison, Gary?"

I replied, "Getting out of the prison is the part of my story that gets interesting."

Brooks moved closer to the edge of his seat and said, "Please continue."

I crossed my legs, leaned back, and said, "Well, in my last year at the prison, there was a lot of out-of-country work for the prisoners. We would be shipped off to either the Philippines or Africa. In the Philippines, we would work on the docks. In

Africa, we would make field bases. We were treated like slaves. We were given minimal food and water."

Brooks, wanting to learn more about my experience, lightly pressed, "How did you handle this type of slave work?"

"To be honest, the slave work was hard. The guards had us working up to eighteen hours without a break. Fifty of us would arrive on sight on a Monday. Only thirty-three returned to the prison. The rest died from exhaustion and disease," I said dejectedly.

Brooks, still being very careful with how he worded questions, asked, "How many people from your team survived?"

I replied in slight confusion, saying, "I really don't know. When I left, Fernsby was the only one at the prison. The last time I saw Weppler and Andrews before I left, they were in the Middle East."

Brooks asked, "Why did they take you away from the prison that one last time?"

"At the time I didn't know. I honestly believed that they were taking me to either another trench or to another harbour. Where they took me was surprising, to say the least," I replied.

Brooks was slightly confused. "Where did they take you, Gary?"

"They took me to a military compound in India. When I arrived, the guards took me to a fairly nice bedroom and left me there. I was in that bedroom, alone, for about three hours, until their superior greeted me. I was trying to figure out why I was there. There wasn't any fighting in India. All of the work in the Indian supply chains was done by the military. They did not utilize slave labour."

"How did you know you were in India?" asked Brooks.

I leaned slightly forward and replied, "Well, when I got in my room, I looked out my window and saw the Indian flag outside. Also, the guards outside had Indian Army uniforms on. Everything I saw suggested that I was in India. But India is a fairly large country, and I just didn't know where in India I was."

Brooks looked at his notes, then looked back up and asked, "You said the superior greeted you… tell me how that conversation went for you?"

I had to lean back into my chair to really remember that conversation. After a few seconds, I remembered it. "The conversation did not go so well for me. The conversation seemed to go quite well but for the CO."

Brooks, absorbed in my story, said, "Please explain that to me."

I sat back and responded, "It was late evening. The sun was about to set. The room was glowing orange from the light of the setting sun. I felt confused and a little angry. I still did not know why I was there. No one seemed to have the slightest inclination to tell me why I was there. I felt like a lost dog, with no sense of smell, looking for home. As I was trying to find my way out of the bedroom, the hallway door opened. Two men point their guns in my face and tell me to get on the floor, and me not wanting to die, I lay face down on the floor."

"'Well, that was easier than I thought it would be. My name is Lieutenant Colonel Madhav Aditya. Call me Madhav. Now, soldier, what is your name?'

I looked up at him and extended my hand to shake his. 'Corporal Gary Foltz of the 22nd Rifle Regiment.'

I was now really confused. Madhav was extending a very cold and formal verbal greeting without providing any emotional warmth to support it. Madhav responded with, 'Pleasure to meet you, Corporal Foltz. Please, walk with me.'

I was confused that they had not yet started beating, or power hosing, me. I quickly decided I should just go along with the charade, at least until I had some idea of whatever was going on. I followed Madhav out of my room.

With an almost imperceptible smirk, Madhav asks, 'You must be wondering why you are here, in a place like this. Am I right?'

I took a second to gather my thoughts. I responded, 'Well, I am wondering what I am doing here, but I do know what I am not here for.'

'Please, Gary, do tell,' asked Madhav. The smirk on his face was now easy to see.

Despite Madhav's smirk, I responded with sheer confidence. I said, 'India doesn't need slave labour to move supplies through. The labour to move supplies is provided by military reserves and national workers. I also know that there are massive factories for Hyena Tech. I did Hyena Tech work back at the prison. Why would the EPC move me here when I could do the same job back in Mongolia?' For some reason I lost my train of thought, so I had to pause.

Madhav, being very patient, pulled out a cigar, lit it, and asked, 'Is that everything, Gary?'

I had successfully recovered my train of thought, so I continued, 'I won't be working as a pack mule since I do not have the body build for it. I know for a fact that I am not in Europe, so I wouldn't be cleaning anything. There, I think I am done. I can't think of anything else I will not be doing. The reasons for my being here can range from teaching kids advanced robotics to cleaning your presidents shoes.'

Madhav chuckled, took a puff from his cigar, and clasped his hands slowly and said, 'Well, Gary, you are full of surprises. I can tell you are smart. That is why you are here. Please follow me.'

I obliged and followed him. I was slightly worried, but he had just told me I was there because someone thought I was smart. I hesitatingly just kept following him."

"Why were you worried about where he was taking you?" asked Brooks.

"Well, he was taking me in the direction of a not-so-appealing building. It was made out of bricks. There were bloodstains on the outside walls. I honestly didn't know what we were doing there," I replied, slightly disturbed.

Brooks got nervously excited about where my story was going to go. He blurted out a chain of questions before he regained control of his curiosity. He asked, "What happened next? What did he make you do? Did he torture you? Did he do something that most people would not think of? Did he do something that most people would consider inhumane?"

While Brooks asked me those questions quickly, I wasn't surprised because of what I had told him about myself to this point.

However, what Madhav had prepared was almost the exact opposite of what Brooks thought Madhav had prepared for me. I actually enjoyed it. What did surprise me, during my stay in India, was what came next.

⌐ CHAPTER 10 ¬
And the Reality of Our Sins

B ROOKS LOOKED DOWN AT his watch and said, "It seems like that's all of the time we have today. I'll see you next Tuesday, same time?"

I replied contentedly, "Yes, of course, Tuesday at the same time."

As I started my walk home, I recognized someone on the sidewalk. It was a man, but not an ordinary man. He was a clown-like man. He drew attention to himself like a coffin in a roomful of barrels. He wasn't lifeless as the word 'coffin' would imply, but everyone around him seemed grim and simple.

As I slowly approached him, I found myself intrigued. I was wracking my brain trying hard to remember where, and when, I had last seen this jester. Where had I seen this comedian, this needle in a world of a haystack? My brain was very definitively working in overdrive, but I just couldn't put the pieces together.

Then I recognized what triggered my memories. Almost at the same time, I saw the scar on his lip and the disfigurement on his hands. The picture became clearer and clearer as we approached each other.

His jacket was worn. The left sleeve of his jacket had enough holes to make it look like Swiss cheese. The right sleeve was held together by duct tape and stitches, which hid his life's battle scars. Life had not been kind to him.

As he and I got closer and closer, I remembered from where I had known him. Now that I had the context, I just had to figure out his name. Who was this man? I recognized him very easily, but my mental block for his name was overpowering. What was this man's name? Why did I think I knew him? Was my mind playing tricks on me again?

At the end of my approach, we both stared at each other in the middle of the walkway. I looked him over, head to foot, as he did with me. How did I know this man? I delved deeper into my archives of memory and remembered that face, that *smirk*. That smirk was a dead giveaway. Standing in front of me was Fernsby.

"Fernsby... is that you?" I asked with slight caution. I needed confirmation, but I also did not want to appear stupid.

He looked at me, distraught. His face also wore slight confusion. He licked and pursed his lips, and then replied, "Who's asking?"

I thought that there wasn't a chance he would remember me. I mean, why would he? We hadn't seen each other for about eight years. Just the same, I attempted to jog his memory and answer him. "It's me, Foltz. Remember, we fought together in BC for two years? We ate dead soldiers and drywall together. We were in jail together in Mongolia for five years." The part about eating dead soldiers and drywall was a very lame attempt at dry humour.

The confused look on his face did not change. He denied knowing what I was talking about. I had my suspicions, but for whatever reason, he wanted me to think that my attempts to jog his memory had failed. What had happened to him?

"What have you been doing for the past ten to fifteen years?" I asked.

He paused to think about my question. Perhaps he needed time to think, because ten to fifteen years was a long time. Perhaps he was genuinely trying to place me somewhere in all the places he had been. From my perspective, I was sure I piqued his curiosity. I was hoping he wanted more information to help him remember me, if he could. He said, "I was on the front lines in the Middle East, Europe, Africa and even in Australia. I am sorry, sir, but I have no recollection of you. And the name 'Foltz' does not help either."

I was surprised that he was so consistently denying knowing me. Apparently my face showed my surprise, and Fernsby simply replied, "Sorry, pal, but you have me confused with someone else."

Okay, if you aren't Fernsby, who are you? So I asked him one last question. "My sincerest apologies, sir. I honestly do not go around stopping people on the sidewalk, fabricating stories that I know them. Just one last question, if you don't mind, now that I know what your name is not – what *is* your name, sir?"

He looked at me with a slight smile and said, "It's not the name you addressed me with, Foltz." Very cryptically, he continued, "There is something deep inside you that you just can't ignore. You can't ignore something deep inside, but you also don't open yourself to others. You let people see the book cover of your life, but you never open the book to let them read the pages." He then walked off into the distance before I could process what he said to me.

Why are we still at war? I (we) represent the old generation. The stranger (they) represents the new generation. We just wanted to protect them from the past mistakes. We never showed the true horrors of the past to them. We just wanted to better their futures. Unfortunately, for better futures, they must experience bad times in order to learn from mistakes that led to bad times. The people who do experience the bad times want desperately to protect those coming after them. The people coming after them have not had the opportunity to learn from mistakes they have not had the opportunity to make.

Battles were fought that shouldn't have been. Lives were lost that shouldn't have been. Generations that led cold, unfeeling lives could have had real lives. This was the sum of our past addends, the quotient of the dividends and the divisors.

I could go on with the metaphors and the excuses, but in the end, we are here because of our past mistakes. We are here because someone wasn't satisfied with what they had. We are here because we never saw a man at the other end of the rifle. We are here because we only saw a monster that wanted to see the world burn. The monster we saw ended up burning everyone.

The saddest part from all of the facts, metaphors, and lies is that life is real. Life is the reality of our sins.

⌐ CHAPTER 11 ¬
Confusion

A FEW DAYS WENT BY after talking to the man on the sidewalk who I thought was Fernsby. He walked like Fernsby. He talked like him and definitely looked like him. But there was something different about him. He just wasn't the same man that I fought alongside in Princeton, or in the north. I thought long and hard about what could be different.

For whatever reason, my brain took me back to my days in Sunday school. The teacher would talk to us about our souls going to Heaven when we die. Maybe death was not the only time when a person's soul can be affected. Perhaps Fernsby's soul was the key? Perhaps what was different about him was how, through his life's battles, his soul got 'damaged' somehow. Perhaps his soul got thrown into a blender. The blender was turned to high and then turned off. Fernsby's soul then got put back together with scotch tape and bubble gum. He certainly seemed to be a man on the verge of snapping from sanity to insanity. But then, sanity and insanity have to do with a person's mind, not their soul. I guess I had some more analysis to do regarding Fernsby.

My curiosity got the better of me, and I researched Fernsby on my computer. I needed to find out if he was officially still alive. All the records I had looked at told me that he was missing-in-action (MIA), but presumed dead. That news severely disheartened me, but I still had other files to read. Another file said that he had disappeared, with hundreds of others, during the northern assaults on Yukon in late September of 2054. Knowing he was still in that dreadful prison, I could only hope for the war to be over soon. With the war over, he and my other squad mates could make it out safely.

The rest of the week passed without incident. I was on my way to Brooks's office for my next appointment. I was quite preoccupied, wondering how Fernsby was doing. Speaking of Fernsby, how were Weppler and Andrews doing? Did Andrews need new parts for his prosthetics? Did Weppler know his family was safe with the National Guard in Texas? Or maybe I should say, what was left of the National Guard!

Did the enemy turn Fernsby into a sleeper agent? The enemy could send a sleeper agent into our society to take down the RUD's army from the inside. I had lots of questions and no one to answer them. Wait a minute, Brooks could answer my questions. I was on my way to see him! With that new realization, I quickened my step a little. I now had a very solid, personal motivation for my session with Brooks.

As I sat in his waiting room, I talked with the other veterans about our experiences in the war. We talked about the places we'd been to, the friends we'd made, and the people we'd lost. I was quite amazed with the age differences of all the vets in the room. I was in my late thirties. The man to my right was twenty-four. He had been honourably discharged due to injury. The man to my left was in his early sixties. He had retired from the army to be with his dying wife. He and his wife had been married for over forty years. They had known each other since childhood. He told me he still remembered the day they met. He knew the day they met that she was the one for him. Listening to him, I got the sense that his wife was his world. He loved her dearly. The thought of trying to carry on without her petrified him!

To the person reading this book, this war brought out the worst in people. Sometimes, though, you have to bring out the worst to find the good in them.

"Mr. Foltz. Dr. Brooks will see you now," said the receptionist.

"Hello, Gary, how have you been since we last met?" questioned Brooks.

"It has been a very eventful week. Thanks for asking," I replied.

"Please have a seat and tell me about your week," Brooks said as he opened his notebook.

I answered, "Well, doctor, I actually have a question for you." I leaned forward and moved to the edge of my seat. I was hoping that the leaning and moving forward would indicate that what I wanted to ask was on a more personal level.

"And what is your question, Gary?" asked Dr. Brooks as he looked up with a sharp smile on his face.

I took a slight pause to gather my words, and then proceeded to speak. "After I left your office last week, I saw a man on the sidewalk who looked like one of my old squad mates from Princeton. When I first saw him, I could not believe my eyes! I looked for identifying features. I found all the identifying features I could remember. I could easily have discounted the encounter if I only found *similar* physical characteristics. But this guy looked to be a carbon copy of my old squad mate. His face, his height, even his scars matched his injuries in Princeton and in prison. But he claimed complete ignorance of who I was talking about. Now, I do have to admit that there was something about him that just wasn't what I remember. My thinking kept going back to his face. His face was exactly as I remembered it but yet not. How can a face do that? Seeing this guy was like seeing a beautiful car and you pop the hood open and there is no engine," I said with morbid confusion.

Brooks sat back and took a deep breath and gave his opinion about my experience last week. "Listen, Gary, I don't want to say that you were seeing things because, knowing you, your PTSD isn't that severe. At least not according to the tests we did on you a few weeks back. You *are* suffering from PTSD, but your symptoms are not severe enough to cause this kind of hallucination. I am going to say that you saw someone who looks like him, but the man you saw wasn't actually him."

I interrupted Brooks right there and stood up for myself. I challenged him, saying, "There is no way somebody looks exactly like Fernsby in that way. There were very few white males in that prison when I left. Fernsby's physical characteristics easily identified him in that prison. Only Fernsby looked like Fernsby, if you are catching my drift."

Brooks, in his attempt to calm me down, replied, "Okay, Gary, there is no need to jump the gun here. Please calm down. Now, take a slow, deep, breath. Can you describe to me what Fernsby looked like, can you do that for me?"

I took a deep breath and said, "Yeah, I can do that." I began to describe Fernsby's personality to Brooks. I knew that Brooks had asked me to describe what Fernsby looked like, but I reasoned that it would be good for Brooks to understand Fernsby. I explained that no matter the situation, Fernsby always had a joke. I told Brooks that Fernsby always had to have the last word and he could always brighten the mood in some way, shape, or form. I remember one time, when strings were chasing us, or another time, knee deep in who knows what, he always had a smile and a positive attitude.

Brooks stood up and went over to get a glass of water at the portable mini bar. His gait told me all I needed to know about what he was going to say to me. He came back with two glasses of water, put them on the coffee table, and said, "You two were really close. I can tell from how you talk about him. He meant a lot to you. I understand that. I had a friend who volunteered to fight. They sent him to Egypt with nine hundred other men and a hundred heavy armoured tanks. I think the tanks were similar to the one your brother drove." Brooks looked at me, thinking I might want to add something, but I didn't, so he continued his story.

"Anyways, they were deployed in early march of '56. They were in Egypt for two reasons. They were to finish the defensive training in Cairo, and to provide backup for the city's defense during EPC attacks. Unfortunately, Cairo's defenses were hideously unskilled. Their defense made the Polish defense in World War 2 look skilled." Brooks paused, took a sip of water, and then continued.

"So, with what little supplies they had, they made a defensive stand that was clearly not prepared for the task at hand. The trenches, if you could call them trenches, weren't dug deep enough. The trenches were more like well-worn paths through the mud and clay. The excuses they had for sandbags all had holes in them. They did not have enough flares or glow-sticks for everyone when the EPC conducted an attack at night. Under normal circumstances, there would be fifty flares and a hundred and twenty glow sticks for every fifty soldiers. The fighting conditions they had were not normal circumstances. They had to ration the flares and glow sticks to eight flares and sixty glow sticks for every hundred soldiers." These conditions made my experience in Princeton look like a walk in the park!

"Anyways, enough about me and my friends, let's continue from where we left off the other day." Brooks said this like he was hiding something, so I tried asking him a question to get more from his story.

I pleaded with him. "What? You can't just tell me one half of the beginning of a story, and then just leave me hanging!" I was hoping for him to continue.

Brooks replied with a smirk on his face. "Oh, yes, I can leave you hanging!" He pointed at me and said, "You're the patient." Then he pointed at himself and said, "I'm the doctor. I control what we talk about. We are not here to talk about me or my friends."

I couldn't argue with his short but valid point, so I asked politely, "Where *did* we leave off, Brooks, I can't remember."

Brooks responded, "About three weeks after your arrival in India, you were teaching kids math and advanced robotics. Khaled approached you after class one day." He was attempting to jog my memory.

I paused briefly. After a few seconds, I recalled the conversation. "Right. When Khaled approached me, I had been teaching mathematics and basic robotics for about one and a half weeks. Academically speaking, Khaled was the brightest kid in the class. My job had three parts to it. My initial job was to teach these kids the theory on how war machines worked. The kids needed to demonstrate the theory about how the machines worked by the time they turned fourteen. They then needed to know how to drive the war machines. By the time they turned sixteen, the kids needed to be skilled at manoeuvring the machines in war-like conditions. No pressure!"

Brooks, slightly surprised by this, asked, "Did your efforts work?"

"They worked, but not without a lot of trial and error. Before my services were 'asked for,' shall we say, out of the first class of a hundred pilots, only two of them were deemed moderately useful. The commanding officers figured the pilots were too young. The officers were correct that the pilots were too young. The officers were also correct that the pilots needed to learn a better understanding for the machines. To do this, the pilots needed a solid foundation in robotics and advanced mathematics; that is how the requirement for my skills arose. The officers took a gamble that someone who had the required knowledge that the pilots needed would also be able to teach. Fortunately for me, I had always had the ability to transfer knowledge, as long as the student was receptive. Sadly, the plan worked," I replied.

Dr. Brooks, slightly confused, straightened up and, wanting clarification, asked, "What do you mean 'sadly'?"

I looked up at him, confused. I could not imagine why he would ask that, but then I remembered he hadn't seen past the front lines of the war. I explained, "The kids that were chosen could have been anything they wanted to be. They could have chosen any vocation, from an astronaut to a zoologist. Instead, they were forced to pilot war machines with enough firepower to take down five skyscrapers. If the pilot was good enough, he could use the machine to destroy an entire city. I've seen these machines snap some of the strongest men I have ever met in half, like toothpicks. Just think of the repercussions of putting this kind of destructive power into the hands of a child. That just made the EPC's offence almost insurmountable, on and off the battlefield! The politicians are merely raising soldiers from birth – something that I want to steer well clear of."

Brooks, being very understanding, said, "Don't worry, Gary, just tell me about teaching the kids math and robotics."

I sighed with relief, knowing that I didn't have to talk about something that truly made my stomach churn. I continued my story about when Khaled approached me after class.

I looked over and saw Khaled approaching me. The second class had ended and I knew he was going to either ask me a question or hope to talk theory. I thought I would initiate the conversation for a change, so I asked him, "Alright, Khaled, what is your question for today? How close is Research and Development to crossing the barrier between cyborg tech-nology and weapons? You do realize that when the barrier between cyborg technology and weapons is crossed, soldiers can have a machine gun for an arm! Or do you want to know where the Hyenas got their groundbreaking technology?"

Khaled gave me a weird, questioning, glare, but asked his daily question as usual. "Where did the Hyenas come from?"

His question caught me off guard. I replied, "Khaled, I went over this a few days ago. The Hyenas are elite military contractors that work for the EPC. They make the machines you will pilot in a few years."

Khaled sighed, disappointed, and countered me with, "Really?! Do you really think I believe the garbage Madhav told you to say? I was hoping you would give me a little credit for being able to see through that smoke screen."

I paused, glanced at the door to make sure nobody was there, and replied to Khaled with a little annoyance. "You are too young to understand what happens outside of your little slice of the world you call home. Now, leave me alone and stop asking me questions after class!" I pointed to the door. I looked toward the door and saw Madhav standing there. His face was painted with fear and disappointment in me.

"Watch your tone, Mr. Foltz!" cautioned Madhav as he looked at me from top to bottom. "You are scaring the child!" Khaled ran out the door faster than I had ever seen him move.

After Khaled ran away, Madhav approached me slowly. He bent down and unlocked the shackles on my ankles. "I see you are agitated, Gary. You haven't been the same since you arrived here two weeks ago. Is…"

I interrupted him without hesitation and corrected him, saying, "Eleven days! I arrived eleven days ago."

Madhav stopped unshackling me and looked up at me. He was very annoyed that I had interrupted him, but I could not have cared less. Madhav's face was beet red in anger and frustration. He very sternly warned me, "Can you please shut up! Stop interrupting me! Didn't your parents ever teach you to be quiet when others are talking?" He paused only briefly but, in my mind, the pause took forever. He looked at me with disappointment and sheer frustration and continued. "Anyways, since I can feel your frustration wanting to explode out of you like an atomic bomb, calm down. Calm down before you tear the compound apart." I followed his advice and forced myself to breathe slower and calmed myself down.

Madhav sighed with relief. Then his usual smile came back. He then told me what we were going to do after supper. "Alright, Gary, you have been working hard and teaching these cadets very well. As a reward for your hard work, I am going to take you out for some fun this evening. How does that sound?"

Not knowing exactly what his definition of 'fun' was, I looked at him with slightly excited concern. I asked him, "What exactly would we be doing?"

Madhav wrapped his arm around me and said, "Walk with me, Gary." He walked me to my room. On the way, he described his plans for the evening. "First, we will go for dinner and eat real food, not the slop food our chefs make. After we have eaten our fill, we will go see girls dance at the festival." With a smirk, he continued, "You will then get to choose which girl you want to be with for the rest of the night. All the girls will be competing to be 'chosen' by you. You will be pleased with whichever girl you choose.

In the morning, we will have breakfast together. We will have time to talk about the night we had. After breakfast, we go back to work. How does that sound to you, Gary?"

I looked at him, very confused. I sincerely thought he was joking and just having fun with me at my expense. I responded with a very hesitant, "Sounds pretty good! We will see what my qualified answer is tomorrow morning."

Later that evening, Madhav came to my room. He had a suit in one hand and a small box of cigars in the other. Now I knew he wasn't kidding. I grabbed the suit and put it on. I stood in front of the want-to-be-mirror and admired how I looked in the suit. I actually looked pretty good! I turned from the mirror, walked out of the bedroom, and joined Madhav to go have fun for the rest of the night.

The food at the restaurant was incredibly delicious! Madhav told me I could eat whatever I wanted and as much as I wanted. Quite a concept to fully embrace! I hadn't had a proper meal since I left home for boot camp eight years before. Manners were forgotten. I pigged out massively. I think I gained at least five pounds. I think I also stretched my bladder. I drank whatever Madhav kept putting in my cup.

Anyways, after I almost killed myself eating and drinking, Madhav and I left the restaurant. We headed to the festival. On our way to the festival, I had to go to the bathroom. I was in the bathroom for what seemed to be an eternity.

We finally got to the festival and it was amazing. Everything about it dazzled my eyes with colour. There were bright and beautiful colours everywhere. The buildings were smartly painted. Even the vehicles shone! The festival music was very conducive to dancing, and the people danced with grace and poise. Everyone was dressed immaculately. The women made me realize that I had not seen a beautiful woman dressed in feminine clothes for a LONG time! Or was my reaction simply because I had not seen a woman dressed nicely for so long? Who knows? Madhav saw the expression of wonderment on my face. He put his arm around me and said, "Before you choose a girl for the night, come with me and have a seat. Let's watch their performance." Madhav's comment made me remember that the women were 'working' women. The women were perfectly aware that their job was to secure a 'date' for the night.

The women did their jobs well. They mesmerized me with their dancing. All of them had talent to burn! The women were working very hard to make my decision as difficult as they could. I almost regretted that I could only choose one girl.

Eventually, one of the women stood out to me like blood on a white towel. She wore a facemask that teased me a little. I wanted to get up and remove it, but I realized that the mask was part of her mystery. She also had tattoos all over her body. The tattoos insinuated that she had secret stories to tell. I wanted to ask her about each one. Her eyes bore into me and broke me perfectly in half. I knew she was the one I was going to choose. The other women did not stand a chance.

I think Madhav sensed I had made my decision and asked me, "Okay, Gary, which girl have you chosen?" I did not hesitate to choose the girl with the facemask and tattoos. When the girl and I were walking up to the room, I heard Madhav yell from behind me with a chuckle, "Have fun, Mr. Foltz. I will see you at eleven-thirty a.m. for breakfast. Oh, and don't be too loud! I do want to be able to sleep tonight." I kind of chuckled, devilishly, to myself.

I was going to tighten my hand on the girl's hand, but I was too late. The girl had already tightened her hand on mine. She looked up at me and flashed her exquisite smile on me. I guessed she knew full well that she was beautiful. She also knew full well exactly how to please a man. She may even know how to please a man in ways the man had never before experienced.

I was quite pleased with myself that I wasn't married. I really wanted to enjoy this woman of mystery without thinking that I was cheating on a wife with whom I had sworn vows to. In the back of my mind, though, was the thought that what was going to happen would disappoint my parents. Mom and Dad were both very conservative in their views on sex and marriage. I shook my head to get my thinking back to the present. The girl and I entered the room and I closed the door behind us. I asked her, "So how are we going to do this?"

She replied by walking up to me. She had a cell phone in her hand. It was ringing. She said, "The call is for you." She handed the phone to me. Then she went to the bathroom conjoined to the room. I was slightly confused about what happened, so I looked at the phone. It was still ringing. I put it to my ear and asked, "Who is this?"

The voice sounded electronically modified. I couldn't make out if I knew the person. The person on the other end of the line said, "You will know who I am when we meet. All you need to know right now is that I am your only ally inside India. I cannot tell you exactly when we will meet. I can say that we *will* meet soon." Then the person behind the voice ended the call.

⌐ CHAPTER 12 ¬
Distant Estate

BROOKS, ABSORBED BY MY story, asked, "What happened next, Gary? Did you have any idea who had called you?"

I replied, "I had some idea that it was a black ops agent working in my area. But because of the voice masking, I could not identify who was on the other end of the line. I suspected the black ops were told to get me out of India. The caller couldn't have been any of my squad mates because they are all in prison or dead. Nor could he have been any of the guys in the Handmaiden's squad. All the guys in her squad died five years ago in the Yukon when we got ambushed. I was clueless about the caller's identity, so I just patiently waited for their arrival.

"I was in the unenviable position of having to put the call out of my mind. I had to rely on him to come to me when the time was right. I couldn't do anything about the call, so I just went to bed."

"What about the woman that took you to your room, what happened between you two?" asked Brooks with a smirk.

Until Brooks asked me about her, I had completely forgotten about her. I replied, "Oh yeah. After she gave me the phone, she disappeared. She left me in the room by myself. Like I said, I just went to bed and had breakfast with Madhav in the morning."

"And how did breakfast go?" asked Brooks.

I tilted my head left and right slightly and smirked. I replied, "It went well. Madhav thought that I had had the time of my life. It was just easier for me to let him think that the dancer had thrilled me. In reality, I had been mentally thrown down the deep hole of an intense chess game and it was my opponent's move. While I was thankful that I had had a good sleep despite the phone call, I was getting anxious that the caller told me we were meeting soon. Unfortunately for me, I could only wait.

"I waited for two very long months for a sign of some kind. One day I was heading back to my room after a class, and I saw a box on my bed. I opened it."

"And?" Dr. Brooks prodded.

I smirked and continued, "There was a note in the box that read, 'ink in the front.' In addition to the note were a handgun with two magazines, a burner phone, some chewing gum, a watch and a ring. I took all of them out of the box and studied the note again. 'The ink in the front.' For whatever reason, the slang term 'ink' came to mind. Could this note be referring to the dancer that disappeared a few months back? And could 'front' be referring to the front of the compound? I was kind of proud of myself for seeming to have unlocked the cryptography! I immediately went to my window and looked to the right at the front gate. My heart sank a little because there was nothing that stood out. I went back to the box, sat down, and thought about the phrase in deeper thought."

Brooks, a little annoyed that my detective skills had failed me, asked, "Did you figure it out? What did ink in the front mean?"

I chuckled at Brooks's annoyance and continued, "The label on the front of the box was imprinted with ink. Every dot on the front of the box was part of a Morse code phrase which, when translated into English, read 'market 1 H.' I understood it as Market, Moreland Incorporated, One Hour. So I prepared to go to Moreland Incorporated in the marketplace in one hour. I went with a required two-man escort.

"My escorts followed me closely all around the marketplace until they lost me. I don't know how they lost me because I certainly was not trying to shake them. Just when I realized I was on my own, I was getting pushed/guided into an alley by people wearing facemasks. I was petrified! Visions of dying a horrible death flew through my mind. Just when I was sure I was going to have a panic attack, the apparent leader came and stood a couple of feet in front of me and paused. The slight panic started and I felt fairly sick. I was getting very anxious. I did not know if the person standing in front of me was a man or a woman. If I were a betting man, I would have bet everything on the person being a man. I could not think of any woman who could command the kind of presence and respect this person did. The leader's mask hid the person's identity completely. Very nervously, I took a quick look at the others. I realized that each of their masks hid their identities perfectly. Then I saw the leader raise his/her hands to the mask to unclip it. Anticipation was killing me – could he/she take any more time to remove that mask?? I was transfixed instantly. My body went from knee-slapping fear to absolute calmness in the smallest fraction of a second! The leader was Handmaiden. I wanted so badly to run and hug her, but she was Handmaiden. She is the one woman I had ever known who could command even greater presence and respect than any man – and she was my friend!"

"'It has been awhile, Foltz, how has it been?" asked Handmaiden while giving her men hand signals.

"'Well, I was in a Mongolian prison for five years with my team, and now I am teaching children how to pilot Hyena war machines, so I've definitely seen better days. How about you? I thought you died during the ambush in the Yukon,' I replied.

⌐ CHAPTER 13 ¬

The Who, the What and the Why

"HANDMAIDEN?? HOW CAN YOU be alive?" I asked in astonishment. "I thought you died during the ambush in Yukon."

Almost flippantly, and with a chuckle, Handmaiden replied, "Yukon? Yeah, we made it out of Yukon quite easily, actually. We also made the EPC soldier wannabes look like teenagers with paintball guns."

Handmaiden understood that I wanted to make sense out of her and her team being there. She, on the other hand, wanted to get on with the task at hand. She explained, almost matter-of-factly, what the task at hand was. "Anyways, my team is working with a small team of SEALS. We are teamed together to cripple the supply depots in the surrounding area.

We are also directed to assassinate the CO's. The working theory is that crippling the supply depots and assassinating CO's will help swing the war in our favour."

As soon as I heard her assignment, I questioned if her assignment would indeed bring the results expected. I asked Handmaiden, "Do you really think that killing some officers and destroying a few supply depots will swing the war in our favour?"

Handmaiden replied, with some annoyance, "Foltz, I'm just following orders. These orders come from the council. Your job is to complete your part of the mission. If the war does not swing in our favour, after we have successfully completed our missions, the people that came up with the plan will have some serious explaining to do."

While I definitely had my doubts about how this plan was going to play out, I was also excited. I was excited because I hadn't seen any action since Yukon. I just needed to know my mission. I stood a little more erect, focussed my eyes on Handmaiden and asked her, "Handmaiden, what do you need me to do?"

Handmaiden gave me step-by-step instructions, similar to how a teacher would instruct a student. I appreciated this approach because there was no room for 'interpretation.'

Wasting no words, Handmaiden replied, "The gum we gave you is made of state-of-the-art explosives. The burner phone we gave you is designed to trigger the explosives. Put the gum where it will attract a lot of attention. Good luck, Gary. It's nice seeing you again."

After Handmaiden gave me those instructions, something slammed me hard in the face and knocked me out cold.

When I awoke, everything looked fuzzy. I saw a clock on the wall. I squinted to see its hands. According to the clock, I had been unconscious for a few hours. I tried to focus my eyes, but my head still hurt from being hit in the face. I was in a hospital bed with what looked to be Madhav sitting in a chair at the end of my bed. He was hunched over, looking down at the floor. His hand was on his forehead. All appearances suggested that Madhav was waiting for me to wake up. I was shocked! How did Madhav know where to find me? The fact that he was there confused the heck out of me!

When I moved my head, Madhav looked at me. He spoke to me with seeming genuine concern. "I know you have had a rocky day, Gary. What happened to you? What happened in the market?"

My hurting head did not help clear my confusion. And Madhav had talked to me in a way that suggested he and his team had just been attacked. When you've been in battle and lived to tell about it, you recognize the tone and manner very quickly. I was shortly to learn that my assessment was correct – they had been attacked.

I wanted to know where I was, so I asked Madhav, "Where am I?"

Madhav replied impatiently, and needlessly loudly, "You are in the infirmary. Now, what happened at the market!"

Madhav yelling at me confused me even more! I needed some time to process what had happened to me. I needed Madhav to shut up, so I lied to him about what happened. "Calm down, Madhav. I'll tell you what happened. I was walking around, minding my own business. I was looking for a souvenir for my nephew back home. Quite spontaneously,

I looked behind me. I was surprised that your men weren't there. I resumed my shopping, and a gang pulled me into an alleyway. They wanted money. After they found out I was practically broke, they knocked me out."

Madhav brought me a glass of water and a cup of pills. Almost reluctantly, he said, "Well, your story does check out from what other sources told me."

My head was starting to clear. Still slightly confused because I did not know what had happened to me after I was knocked out, I asked, "What *did* happen at the market, Madhav?"

He pulled his chair beside my bed and told me what he knew about the attack. "From what my sources say, the gang was actually a group of resistance fighters. The fighters were wearing street clothes and had old weapons. They started their attack by using small, remotely detonated explosives in and around the supermarket. After the explosives had been detonated, the fighters moved with speed and coordination. I think they were ex-military, maybe even ex-Special Forces."

His hypothesis astounded me. I did my best to hide my surprise. I needed to do or say something that would take his attention away from my face. I volunteered, "Do you mind if I look at the video feed from the attack? I have worked with Special Forces before. I might be able to give you my opinion on who I think they are." I really didn't want Madhav to trace the attack back to me or Handmaiden and her team. My plan was to give Madhav bad intelligence. I had to figure this out because the intelligence had to be legitimate enough to send him and his team on a wild goose chase but at the same time immediately discount me as purposely lying to them.

Madhav looked at me. I could tell he was thinking hard about my proposal. He stood up, walked over to the door to leave, and turned halfway around and addressed me. "I will talk to my staff about your proposal. I will return and tell you when we come to a decision."

I was stuck in my infirmary room for so long, I thought I was going to go stir crazy! When Madhav finally returned, I truly thought I had been in that room for at least a month.

Madhav walked into my infirmary room and said, "Gary, my fellow officers and I have come to a decision." When he continued, I looked up at him with a sigh of relief. "We have decided that you will work with us to break down the surveillance tape. We will continue to work together to trace the gang back to their base. Now, get out of bed, make yourself presentable, and come with me to the film room."

On our way to the film room, we exited the infirmary. Exiting the infirmary, we were in the main yard of the compound. I looked around and saw signs that India was preparing for something big.

From what I could recall from recent memory, the yard had at least twice the manpower I had previously seen. Semis were unloading an inordinate number of Draugrs and Minotaurs. I was scared for Handmaiden's team because they were not equipped for this type of heavily equipped opposition. Somehow, I had to warn them.

The technicians' building was on the other side of the main yard from the infirmary. As Madhav and I entered it, Madhav began to explain to me what I had seen in the yard. "I know you are wondering what you saw out in the yard. What you saw was just a small fraction of a trillion-dollar weapons and equipment shipment. Small parts of the shipment are being off-loaded around the world to help our men on the front lines."

I had to appear nonchalant and doing so was not easy! I knew he and his people were our enemy. What I had seen in the yard was enough firepower to overthrow a country in a matter of days. Handmaiden and her team had to be told that weapons and equipment were being off-loaded around the world. She needed to know that she had a lot of very tough battles ahead of her.

"Alright, Gary, welcome to the film room," said Madhav. He seemed rather pleased with himself as he opened the door. He presented the room like a used-car salesman, snake smile and all.

The room was about the size of an elementary-school classroom, but that is definitely where the similarities stopped. In addition to Madhav's team, the film room had high-tech surveillance equipment of every description, and a small armoury. In my opinion, the equipment and the armoury were state of the art.

Madhav immediately started to brief me and his team. "Gary, this is my team. You and my team will be working together for the next several days. Let me introduce you to them."

Pointing out his team, from left to right, he said, "Borris is a Russian surveillance technician. He has been working in surveillance for eight years. Beside him is Saksham. Saksham is a local surveillance tech. He has been working in surveillance for twelve years. Gary, please walk over to the right of Saksham."

Madhav gave us our working orders. "The three of you are now one team. The three of you will eat, sleep, and work in this room for the next fifteen days."

Madhav then gave us his instructions for our facilities. "Your beds will be here within the hour. There is a washroom behind that door over there. If you need anything, use the landline. Good luck, gentlemen. I will see you in fifteen days. Are there any questions?" Madhav made very brief eye contact with each of us. "Okay, I will assume that my instructions have been sufficient. Like I said, I will be back in fifteen days. I fully expect to see concrete results from your efforts." Madhav left with haste, insinuating, at least to me, that he did not want to give us time to formulate questions that he was sure he would not know the answer to. I think Madhav would equate not knowing an answer to weakness. The last thing Madhav wanted to communicate to us was weakness, so he just about ran out of the room.

When Madhav left the room, Borris and Saksham stood up. Borris went to close the door. Saksham held out his hand, saying, "Corporal Foltz, it is nice to finally meet you. We are your handlers until we hand you over to Handmaiden."

I did not expect Borris or Saksham to mention, let alone know, Handmaiden. I was so confused I almost blacked out. To avoid this, I forced myself to ask a question. "Who are you guys, really?"

Borris chuckled and said, "I wish I could tell you who we are. We *can* tell you two things. First, we definitely aren't whatever that guy said we are. Second, we are your handlers until we hand you over to Handmaiden."

I proceeded to give each of them a hard stare-down. I needed to know if they were toying with me. After my stare-downs, I concluded, for now, that Borris and Saksham were neither my ally nor my enemy. That put me in a desperate position because I did not know which, if either, of the two could be trusted.

┌ CHAPTER 14 ┐
Jousting with Snails

TODAY IS DAY 724 in my five-year contract as a Mimic.

My partner and I have made contact with the VIP Corporal Gary Foltz. We told him we are his handlers. He responded with confusion and doubt. I suspect he thought we were lying. Borris and I will work to slowly gain Foltz's trust.

For the next fourteen days, Borris and I will follow protocol 74-T with Foltz. If Foltz tries to escape, or harm either of us, we will instigate protocol 18-C alongside protocol 74-T.

Under protocol 18-C, the armed guards will take necessary action in the event of the VIP trying to escape or harm either of us. Borris and I cannot be aggressors; it would blow our cover.

Only as a last resort will we switch from protocol 18-C to one of the three following protocols: 94-F, 18-A, and 44-D.

If we have to invoke protocol 94-F, 18-A, or 44-D, Borris and I will stay in disguise.

If we get caught and the enemy try to break us during interrogation, we will use our default identities, and invoke protocol 1-A.

My name is Kyle "Saksham" Yung. I am Mimic 14-D.

Signing off until the next data entry.

Today is day 726 in my five-year contract as a Mimic.

Borris and I seem to have gained VIP Foltz's trust. Foltz is now engaging with us in conversation and helping us do our job as "surveillance techs."

We attempted to invoke protocol 74-T, but Foltz did not respond. Because Foltz did not respond to protocol 74-T, Borris and I decided to invoke protocols 78-T and 82-T. Foltz is responding quite well to both 78-T and 82-T and warming up to Borris and I.

The next twelve days, until Day 0, should be relatively smooth sailing.

My name is Kyle "Saksham" Yung. I am Mimic 14-D.

Signing off until the next data entry.

Today is day 407 in my five-year contract as a Mimic.

I have completed the mission. The mission was costly! Five of the six teams assigned to this mission have been completely neutralized. I am the sole survivor of the sixth team. My partner, Abraxas, aka Mimic 13-D, was KIA at 1714 hours today.

To complete the mission, I meet up with G7K3 for the drop off. If any problems arise in the next seven days, I will follow protocols 14-A and 17-B.

My name is Kyle "Saksham" Yung. I am Mimic 14-D.

Signing off until the next data entry.

Today is day 428 in my four-year contract with Mimic Corporation.

I am exhausted. I am exhausted because all my partner and I have been eating are MRE's and an occasional apple. Despite eating a miserable diet, our mission has been going smoothly.

The VIP has been complying with our instructions. In ten days, we will be done setting up for the final phase.

Since Saksham and I became a team, 300 days ago, we have been working well together. As a team, we have successfully completed over a dozen missions. We have been working like a well-oiled machine.

My name is Noah "Borris" King. I am Mimic 11-F. Signing off until the next data entry.

Today is day 433 in my four-year contract with the Mimic Corporation.

My partner, Saksham, and I have completed all tasks five days prior to the night of our escape. So we will begin to follow through with protocol 21-A.

Protocol 21-A dictates that we walk the VIP through the mission, from the beginning to the end. The end being us arriving at the drop off. But if things go south, Saksham and I will have to take the VIP to Norway ourselves.

My name is Noah "Borris" King. I am Mimic 11-F.

Signing off until the next data entry.

Today is day 381 of my four-year contract with the Mimic Corporation.

I am working alone on a mission designed for four people. Today is my sixtieth day working alone. But overall I have been on this mission for 184 days.

I am sleep deprived.

I am going to go tap into radio communications after this data entry.

Since I am alone, I have followed through with protocols 11-A and 7-B. Unfortunately, my superiors haven't sent help because of reasons I do not know.

I don't remember if I documented the deaths of my team-mates or not. To be sure my teammates' deaths are documented, though:

- Mimic 14-C; Abram; KIA day 99 on mission; cause of death: the boats.
- Mimic 5-B; Henry; KIA day 63 on mission; cause of death: poisoned.
- Mimic 4-B; Benji; KIA day 39 on mission; cause of death: gunshot wound.
- Mimic 1-A; Reece & Mimic 20-C; Sophia: went to the messenger's cabin on day 118 to get orders or reinforcements. They have not been seen for 66 days. I am declaring that Reece and Sophia are KIA.
- Mimic 9-A; Jules; KIA day 124 on mission, cause of death: public execution.

My name is Noah "Borris" King. I am Mimic 11-F.

Signing off until the next data entry.

Today is day 435 of my four-year contract with the Mimic Corporation.

We are getting close to day 0. Since we invoked protocol 21-A with the VIP two days ago, it seems like he knows what he is doing. The only way for us to know for sure if he knows what he is doing is to see how he reacts when the bullets start flying.

I only want two things out of this mission. The first thing I want out of this mission is for the VIP to get home. The second thing I want is for our side to suffer minimal casualties (I do NOT want a repeat of what happened in Peru).

My name is Noah "Borris" King. I am Mimic 11-F.

Signing off until the next data entry.

Today is day 737 of my five-year contract with the Mimic Corporation.

Tomorrow is day 0 of the mission. We are prepared for day 0. I just confirmed with the ground team that they are prepared to execute the assault tomorrow. The assault will give us the window to raid the armoury and then get to the drop off.

I don't know what it will be like in the streets of Mumbai tomorrow night, but I always prepare myself for the worst.

My name is Kyle "Saksham" Yung. I am Mimic 14-D.

Signing off until the next data entry.

⌐ CHAPTER 15 ¬
The Domino Effect

"SO, GARY, TONIGHT WAS the night you were going to escape… tell me how it all went down," said Brooks.

I had to recall what it was like to run between two sets of opposing gunfire. The gunfire would be between two sides, both of which were heavily equipped for war.

I answered, "It was an experience I can't really describe to you. My best comparison would be like standing sideways between two heavyweight boxers in their match. Both boxers are constantly throwing punches. With punches coming from both sides, avoiding a punch coming from one side means being blindsided by a punch coming from the other side. The one strategy to use is threefold:

- Keep your eyes focussed on where you need to go
- Keep your feet moving in that direction as fast as you can, and

- Do your best to ignore/absorb the punches as you go.

You know that you are likely going to be hit. Your job is to concentrate only on getting to where you need to be. Getting to where you need to be is the only way to escape the assault."

Brooks leaned back, crossed his legs, and said, "Like all other stories, Gary, please start from the beginning."

"Well, before I do that, I want to explain that there are really two aspects to the story. The first aspect is what Borris, Saksham, and I experienced before we left the compound. I guess you could say this aspect was the psychological point of view. The second aspect explains where we ended up physically. Explaining where we ended up physically brings the story closure."

I began with, "We were waiting in the film room for the assault to start. Just waiting in the film room was intense. I could have cut the tension in the room with a dull blade! We were so quiet I could hear my heart beating. Nothing, and no one, not even Saksham or Borris, could have prepared me for what happened next."

"'Are you ready, Gary?' asked Saksham with slight concern in his voice. In a very determined voice, Saksham warned me, 'Just be prepared for anything! This will get scary, *fast*!'

Saksham's comment was the last thing I needed to hear! I was already very nervous and scared, but said, 'As ready as I'll ever be.'

"Saksham and Borris looked at me as if their lives depended on me being ready. In an attempt to calm me down a little, Borris asked, 'Do we need to walk you through the plan again?'

"I waved the back of my hand as if to dismiss their concerns. This was my best attempt to assure Borris and Saksham that I was ready to go. I replied, 'No. Don't worry about me. I've got this. All I have to do is follow you guys and cover my six. In basic training, the instructors hammered into us that we only have one job to do. My one job is to do only my job. Worrying about someone else is not my job. Doing my job is second nature to me. Don't worry, I will do my job, but only my job.'

"From their body language, I knew that Borris and Saksham were experiencing paranoia. Their paranoia manifested in fidgetiness, checking the clock constantly, and Borris tapping his foot.

"From their persona, on the other hand, I knew that Borris and Saksham were top-tier professionals. Top-tier professionals are the best of the best. They are trained to stay calm in extremely intense situations. However, whatever was going to happen next, something they were not telling me, *some*thing had even these guys rattled, but good! I sensed that whatever Borris and Saksham were anticipating was going to make the night a night for the history books.

"The tension in the film room grew as the hours became minutes and the minutes became seconds. All three of us tried in vain to nullify the tension by biting our nails, letting our teeth chatter, or letting our legs shake. I sensed that this could be my last night on earth. Strangely, I did not find this realization surprising at all. Why should I find that realization surprising? I had been fighting for my life for the past eight years. I had gotten kind of used to fighting for my life, after having knocked on death's door as often as I had.

"We were waiting in the film room for our signal to make our way to the armoury. There was dead silence between the three of us. Then a sound I will never forget made its presence known. A deafening, shrill, siren assaulted the air around us. The siren got closer. When it found its target, it shook the city. Afterwards, all three of us heard the whole base mobilizing. Minotaurs rose up, Valkyries took flight, and Draugrs assembled by the hundreds. So many mechanized armaments were deployed, it seemed like both the air and the land were moving.

"The night was truly animated. That night was best described as a domino effect that started when one machine knocked down the next, and so on. The three of us realized that, in our position, we would be considered another domino. We looked like we were just waiting to be knocked over.

"I could only think of two reasons for the type of mobilization we had witnessed. Either the mobilization was for a complete drill, or they were going to be attacked. Considering how fast they were moving and how much machinery was moving, we reasoned they were going to be attacked.

"We were waiting for the signal to move. We had to wait for the 'domino' beside us to fall, which lent a small distraction for us to start our escape. Then the siege of Mumbai began with a bombardment of artillery. We tried to figure out where the artillery was coming from, but in the darkness of night, that effort was futile. All we knew was that it was time to move. Being able to use the enemy's offensive manoeuvre to further distract attention from our escape was incredibly paramount.

"As we were moving through the compound, you could hear the echoes of the battle outside. I was now very thankful that Borris and Saksham had insisted on me rehearsing my escape plan until I was sick of it. My mistake, I was not just sick of rehearsing the escape plan, I was beginning to have nightmares about it! Now, when I needed to rely on the plan, I could not help but recall every detail:

- Survive the siege;
- Survive the crossfire of thousands;
- Escape to Canada; and
- Persevere to the end.

"The ultimate objective was impossible to complete without help. The help I needed came from Saksham and Borris. They were invaluable in getting me out of the city unscathed, with very little aid.

"Now I want to talk about the physical aspect and bring closure to the story. When Saksham, Borris, and I heard the compound mobilizing, we immediately prepared to break out of the film room. We crouched behind the door ready to run for our lives to the armoury. We waited for what seemed to be hours to make our break. When we did breach the door, our feet felt like they were powered with jet engines. We got to the armoury in what seemed to be seconds.

"As we crossed the courtyard, I looked up and saw the largest battle I had ever seen. There seemed to be thousands of Valkyries flying above. The Valkyries were aligning to face the attacker's air force. I could hear the Minotaurs, and other heavy armour, cruising down the streets. The mechanized equipment was getting ready to defend against whatever set foot in the city. The gods of Olympus could have landed on the beach and the EPC defenders wouldn't have so much as flinched. The EPC presented by the Minotaurs, and the other armour seemed impenetrable. The only flaw in the defense was that they didn't know what was on the other side. I was on the same page as the EPC… because I didn't know either!"

⌐ CHAPTER 16 ¬
Heavy Weights

"WHO ATTACKED THE CITY soldiers, Gary?" Dr. Brooks asked.

From Dr. Brooks's tone and body language, I knew he was voicing concern about my well-being when the city soldiers had been attacked. While I appreciated his concern, I looked at Brooks with frustration and answered, "Brooks, the question was not WHO attacked the city soldiers! The true question about the attack was WHAT attacked them."

Brooks's face changed to slight annoyance but also keen interest. He was annoyed because he felt I was splitting hairs with the technical difference between 'who' and 'what.' Brooks continued, "Alright then, *what* was attacking the city soldiers?"

I looked at Brooks and then at the floor. I just realized that I did not have an answer for him. Slowly I answered, "I... don't know."

The slight annoyance that Brooks displayed when he felt I was splitting hairs now grew into full agitation! "What do you mean, you don't know?" he demanded. "You were right there! How could you not know?"

Now I got agitated. I replied, "I mean… I got knocked out. Ok! I got knocked out. Something hit me hard and everything went black. When I woke up, all I saw were scraps of Valkyrie suits, dead bodies, and roaring fires. The compound was ablaze. I could sense that I was moving, but how was I moving? I could feel my feet being dragged over the ground. I struggled to make sense of what was happening to me. Somehow I realized that Borris and Saksham were dragging me out of the compound."

Brooks, clearly baffled from what I had told him, said, "Please tell me about the attack outside of the compound. For instance, did you experience pure chaos the whole time, or did the intensity of the attack gradually increase to total mayhem?"

I grabbed my glass of water, took a drink, and answered with a grin. "Well now, that's where this story gets truly interesting."

Quite unexpectedly, I was fully awake, and was able to run on my own. We were running down the streets at full sprint. The neighbourhood was remarkably quiet, considering that an intense battle was so close.

The main front of the battle was on the beaches but moving quickly. The battle was moving towards downtown fast. No matter how fast we could run, the battle was going to overtake us. We knew that we were going to have to fight for our lives again.

When the fight finally surrounded us, there was no warning. Both sides of the battle seemed to just appear right before us. We were just going down the street and a helicopter hit the ground in front of us and slid down the street for about a hundred feet. Almost immediately, we saw what seemed to be an endless number of tanks driving straight into the fray.

The battle grew in intensity. We saw infantry and machinery going into, and coming out of, battle. The three of us looked at each other and realized that getting out of the city was going to require nothing short of a miracle! The thought of our escape requiring a miracle to get out of the city did not really scare me, because I already knew that I really did not have any right to be alive as it was!

The tanks had driven past us only a few minutes ago. We knew that the EPC forces saw us. The soldiers pursued us as we attempted to flee. We tried to escape but we were outgunned and outnumbered. Slowly but surely, the EPC cornered us. We had nowhere to go. We had to think on our feet. We had to think of where to go that they would not be able to track us down. Saksham took the lead. He led us into the sewers to give us another chance to get out of the city. The sewers were our only hope.

Saksham's plan to get us out of the city worked. We had given the enemy the slip. We could not believe our luck! We had managed to elude them. What was the probability of that? Our fortune seemed too good to be true. Then we heard a distant rumble. We all looked in the direction the rumble had come from. We saw a light at the end of the tunnel, but it wasn't the light of day. It turned out to be the headlights of an oncoming train.

We had seconds to find a way to get out of the way of the train. The train's headlight briefly reflected off something metallic. I jumped up and grabbed at whatever that metallic thing was; it was a manhole ladder. The ladder was solid.

Borris and Saksham were right behind me as I climbed the ladder. The three of us were on the ladder when the train screamed by. Ready or not, we had to continue to the next step of the escape. Borris climbed up to the manhole and poked his head out. He immediately retreated and said, with fear in his eyes, "Ok, there might be a slight problem with what's above."

Saksham asked, "And what would that slight problem be?"

Borris continued with sheer fear, "We are directly under the front lines, also in the wide open. We are going to have to run like our lives depend on it, because they do!

Saksham was shaken. Each time we escaped one problem we had run into another. Even though he was shaken, Saksham remained visually composed. He began to formulate a plan. "What do we have for utility, guys? I have a few stuns and one frag grenade."

Borris added, "I have two smokes."

I checked my pockets and pulled out the items I got from Handmaiden. I reported to Saksham, "I have a pack of chewing gum, a burner phone, a watch, and a ring."

Both Borris and Saksham looked at my utility items like they fit perfectly into Saksham's plan. I couldn't picture how my stuff fit, but they did, and that's all that mattered.

"Give me the phone and gum pack," Saksham said immediately.

I handed the items to him and watched him work. Saksham broke the phone in half, pulled two wires from where the two halves had joined, and stuck them into the pack of gum. He folded the phone's keypad on the top screen in half and pressed the gum pack on to the back of the bottom half. He pressed the three together like a sandwich and pulled what looked like double-sided tape out of the side of the phone. Saksham wrapped the tape around the whole device, leaving the bottom of the phone open so he could use some of the buttons. Saksham looked at me and said, "You know, Gary, these things you had may have just saved our lives."

Saksham handed the device to Borris, who pitched it through one of the holes in the manhole cover. I was still trying to figure out what the contraption Saksham made was supposed to do for us. Fortunately, the only thing that mattered was that the contraption did what Saksham wanted it to. I was also trying to figure out what roles the ring and the watch were going to play in our escape.

There was no time for me to further contemplate escape roles! After Borris threw the contraption through the manhole cover hole, we were climbing out of the manhole and making a run for it. We ran until we had no cover left – about six blocks. Again, we had to think on our feet.

The frantic brainstorming we were engaged in was slowly starting to take a toll on my handlers. Borris's hand was shaking. Saksham was clearly on the verge of a panic attack. I had no choice but to step up and find a way out.

I looked to the left and then to the right. I saw a few quads sitting on the other side of the alley. The quads had just become our escape plan! I showed Borris and Saksham the quads. In a mad dash, each of us ran to a quad, started it, and drove with reckless abandon. Getting the quads going happened so fast, it seemed to be one motion. Borris and Saksham led the way. I followed them, hoping they had found the way out of this warzone.

As we drove down the city streets, the battle intensity grew exponentially. Bullets from both sides were flying over our heads. Minotaurs were around every corner. Exploding artillery destroyed the ground beside me. Skyscrapers were falling. This city was being ripped to shreds.

⌐ CHAPTER 17 ¬
The Beginning of the End

B ROOKS STEADILY PACED AROUND the room. He was trying to wrap his mind around what happened in India two years ago. He suddenly stopped, leaned on the back of his chair, looked at me, and asked, "Gary, can you tell me why the siege of Mumbai happened?"

I give Brooks a squinted stare and replied, "Why? Haven't you been keeping up with recent history?"

Brooks replied with spunk, "Yes. As a matter of fact, I have. I just want you to summarize it, in your own words."

I knew I would have to concentrate to get the story correct. I adjusted my position to sit upright, then began to summarize the fifteen-day Siege of Mumbai.

"Well, for a long time, the RUD knew Mumbai was a critical checkpoint for food, weapons and ammo. The RUD also knew a lot of the weapons were going to the North African and Eastern European front lines. Knowing this, the RUD wanted to disrupt the EPC's supply chain. But they didn't have the manpower to spearhead the operation. So they turned to their allies in Africa to lend over a couple of infantry divisions. The African armies ended up sending over 98,000 men.

"The African armies were very close friends with the world powers of America, EU, and Britain. Despite being from a third-world continent, the African armies always stepped up to help their friends when they could. Mostly by sending them food and water. When the RUD told the African armies that Mumbai was one of the main links in the supply chain, the armies did not hesitate to step up. They immediately sent 98,000 troops to aid the attack on Mumbai.

"Europe and America knew Africa did not have the technology to attack Mumbai, let alone the whole country of India, so they provided the air and land support piloted by 46,000 men and women."

Brooks looked at me both sternly and yet with compassion. He knew I wasn't telling him my personal opinion of the siege. He leaned towards me and said, "Gary, we aren't going to get anywhere if you don't tell me how you felt about the siege."

I then told him what I truly thought about the Siege of Mumbai. "I think it was necessary for the RUD to make some sort of offensive move in the war. Unfortunately, I also think the generals' strategy to approach the city was ineffective and a waste of lives."

Dr. Brooks, very interested in my opinion, said, "Please elaborate on what you mean by 'waste of lives.'"

I explained, with malice, "What I mean is, the generals sent troops blindly into battle with very little dependable intelligence on both the enemy and the layout of the city."

Brooks immediately stood up and attempted to stop me from losing my cool and responded, "No need to get mad or upset, Gary. There was absolutely nothing you could have done to change what the generals did. The generals' strategy was completely beyond your control."

I shot a piercing stare at Brooks. I snapped back at him, "You know what, Brooks, it seems like I have not had control over anything that has happened in my life. I don't think there is one blasted thing that I have done that I had control over! From my mother's death to running across the world! Tell me one thing that was in my control, Brooks. Tell me just one thing! I'll bet there hasn't been one thing in my life that I have chosen to do. I'll bet that there hasn't been one thing in my life that I have chosen to do for me!"

Brooks just stood there. He was not sure where to take the conversation. He was trying to think of something to say that would completely surprise me. I remained seated where I was, continuing to stare at him. I was pretty sure I had laid out my case logically. I was also sure that Brooks knew I had laid out my case well. I could not see a way for him to swerve his way out of my challenge.

Surprisingly, when Brooks did speak, I realized that he had found a crack in my seemingly flawless challenge. He replied, "What about your father, Gary? You could have moved into your own place, but you decided to move back home. Why is that?"

Brooks's question stunned me. I was stunned by how effectively he was able to think on his feet. This also annoyed me to some degree, because Brooks had not given me any time to silently gloat over my, now lost, victory. So I replied, "I moved back in with him because I didn't want him to be alone." Just before I answered Brooks, I thought I was going to say something I believed was expected of me. After I answered Brooks, I realized that what I said was true. It was pure and simple truth. Nothing about my statement was coerced or forced.

My statement made Brooks knowingly suspicious. "Come on, Gary, is that really the reason you moved back in with your father?" He knew I was hiding the truth not from just him… but from myself.

I began to tear up and my throat hardened. I hesitated on my reply. I had to answer Brooks with the truth. I knew that verbalizing the truth would help me continue to recover from my traumatic experiences. I replied, "I moved back in with him for two reasons. I really didn't want to be alone anymore, and I wanted to have someone in my life who genuinely cared for me."

Brooks nodded and replied, "Although I cannot identify with your experiences, I do understand what you are saying. My best advice for you, Gary, would be to become the person you always wanted to be. Become the person you dreamed about being before you went to boot camp, before you entered the world of the depraved, before the world decided to take a walk into insanity."

I was listening very carefully to Brooks. I wanted to see if he was trying to tell me something without saying it. The first thing, or rather, person, that came to mind was Kendall

Wilson. I was rather surprised, because I really did not think that Brooks was referring to her.

"Are you saying I should go and meet up with Kendall Wilson… the journalist I threw over my shoulder in the middle of a supermarket?!" I was more than slightly confused but I actually understood where Brooks was coming from. Truth be told, I did want to delve deeper into the 'Kendall Wilson' topic with Brooks. I wanted to know how much effort I would have to invest in myself to be, and *feel*, human again. In fact, I not only *wanted* to know, I *needed* to know how hard the journey back to feeling human would be. I feared that if I did not know what the journey would entail, and start on it, I would join the world in their jaunt of madness.

⌐ CHAPTER 18 ¬
The Curse of Sleep

A S I LAY AWAKE late at night, sleep escaped me. I just tossed and turned, trying to find that ever-elusive comfortable position that would enable my mind to relax into dreamland. But dreamland was craftier than me. Dreamland continued to dodge all of my efforts. When I did, momentarily, slip into dreamland, I never stayed for long. Dreamland, being the birthplace of many life creations, inventions, and decisions, is exhilarating. On the other hand, Dreamland, being the birthplace of so many events, is also bewildering.

Dreamland seems like it can create life itself. It also seems as though it can recreate the horrors of the dreamer's life. Dreamland, when it recreates the horrors of the dreamer's life, is also known as a nightmare. Many people pretty much ignore their nightmares like they ignore a paper cut. They jump out of bed, walk around for a bit, maybe have a drink of water, and then go back to bed. For people like me, the exception is the rule. When I consider all the horrors I have experienced, there is no way to minimize such experiences.

I have spoken to others with experiences similar to mine who also have the curse of sleep. The best way I can describe the curse of sleep to you is, we fear falling asleep. We know that when we fall asleep, we will again see, hear, and feel that which is impossible to undo.

All of us survivors, knowing that we must sleep to survive, have found a way to sleep. Some survivors use sleeping pills. Some others depend on meditation to sleep. For the unlucky few like me, for whom pills and meditation are not effective, we relive our horrific experiences every night. Each time we relive our experiences, we slip further and further away from society. As we do, we slide into an alienated state of mind.

For whatever reason, I started thinking about which horrors my brain would recall for me to relive. Was it going to be Princeton, Mongolia, Kabul, Norway, Mumbai, Russia, or one of the other countless cities and countries I had been in? My question would soon be answered. Mental fatigue started to win the war for control over my consciousness as I fitfully drifted off to sleep.

I sat up in a field of ash, a wasteland of sorts. I looked to my left. I looked to my right. Very quickly, I realized I was sitting in what used to be a city. I looked further away and I saw skyscrapers in various stages of collapse. There were skyscrapers leaning precariously, some leaning on one another. Still other scrapers had succumbed to gravity and were simply lying on the streets in mountains of rubble.

I got on my feet and began to walk through the streets. I saw the remains of soldiers and military vehicles. I began to approach a toppled building. As I made my approach, I started to hear a faint plea for help. I heard someone yelling, "Help! I'm trapped. Can anyone hear me? Can anyone help me?"

From the voice, I knew the plea came from a boy. My first thought was 'How could a boy have possibly survived this battle?' Not knowing what state he was in, I rushed into the wreckage to try and find him. I encouraged the boy to keep talking so I could follow his voice. I followed the boy's voice to his location. I found him. Technically, I found his hands. He was buried under a pile of heavy rubble. Everything, except his hands, were buried under the rubble. The boy's hands were waving around, trying to attract attention. Poor kid! I could tell he was frightened. I would be frightened too if I were in his situation. Lord knows, I was frightened just from the scene around me, but I wasn't buried under the rubble.

I quickly started to dig him out of the debris he was under. I could not understand how he was still alive. This city had been destroyed years ago. This child should be dead. Despite the apparent logic contradiction, I kept on digging him out.

When I got the last part of heavy debris off the boy, he looked at me, smiled, and said, "Now do it in real life." He then pushed me backward. I fell over into the floor like it was water. I was shocked. It did not make sense. I was drowning in solid matter. I had to find the surface to breathe!

As a person can only do in a dream, I floundered in the ground, trying to find the surface. My body started to cry out for air. I was suffocating. The liquid mud and dirt had a stranglehold on me. I couldn't see at all. The mud and dirt felt like it was solidifying around me. I could barely move. With my lungs screaming for air, I accepted that this time I was not going to cheat death. As I started to lose consciousness, my body relaxed.

I sensed death closing in on me, life slipping away. Death was enveloping me. Death was just about to claim me when I felt my whole body being pulled mercilessly. The pulling force was irresistible. Even the hold that death had on me could not overpower the force. I felt my body being released from the mud and dirt. Frantically, I took deep gasps of air. My lungs, starved for air, filled every air-starved crevasse with every breath. Life had reclaimed me from death's grip.

I surfaced and awoke. That dream had seemed overwhelmingly real! I was lying on my back in an alley. Borris looked down at me with a slight grin and said, "We aren't losing you that easily." He then proceeded to jog down the alley. He was careful to check his corners.

I got up and stood there, frozen. My dream had disoriented me. I wondered where I was and what was happening around me. I scanned the area quickly. I saw skyscrapers on fire. Aircraft were falling from the sky. I heard men screaming, but I couldn't tell if their screams were out of fear or pain.

Someone spun me around. I was face to face with Saksham. He was shaking me to help me get my bearings. He was yelling, "Foltz, we have to move. The buildings are collapsing!" He then pointed up. I looked up. The buildings on both sides of us were falling towards each other. We were between the two collapsing skyscrapers. I had recovered from my dream and the shock of the battle I was caught up in. My instincts kicked in, and we immediately ran for our lives down the alleyway.

Pieces of both buildings were falling all around us. To make matters worse, some of the pieces were on fire!

As we neared the street, the light got progressively dimmer as the alley closed in on our heads. I could not figure out what was happening. Borris and Saksham had awakened me from my dream, and yet as we got nearer to the street, the alley was closing in on us. Nothing was making sense. Maybe, when death comes unexpectedly, mental faculties go haywire. Maybe death really was not going to be cheated after all.

I awoke in a cold, thick sweat, screaming. My head was pounding. My heart was racing. My father rushed into my room, shook my shoulders, and comforted me. "You are okay, Gary. It was just a dream, Gary. That was years ago… you are safe now."

My emotions got the better of me. I started crying. My father wrapped his fatherly arms around me while I bawled on my bed. Dad's embrace was so comforting. I cried even harder, thanking God for such a loving father.

Not knowing if I could adapt to current society because of my past, I also wondered if society would accept the new war-damaged Gary. I was not who I was when I was in society, and society had changed since the war had started. I knew that the only attitudes and actions I could control were my own. I knew that being assimilated back into society was up to me. I had to adapt, but how did I do that? Did I make a plan or go with the flow? Since I only had control over myself, going with the flow seemed like the logical choice.

I woke up the next day worried about what life would throw my way. Would life throw a brick in my face, or would life have a child tell me that my hands looked funny?

I go about my normal routine. I shower, eat breakfast, and go for a walk for some exercise. After my walk, I return home and draw up war-machines plans in my office. The war-machine plans can be used in the future, if needed.

I do have a weekly appointment with Dr. Brooks. My appointment is for me to debrief what has happened to me over the past twelve years. I look forward to my debriefing sessions because I get to tell someone about what keeps me up at night. Debriefing is a critical step in my psychological recovery. I would tell my father but, since Mom died, he pretends the war is over; sometimes Dad even insists that the war never happened. Being an army veteran, I worry about him more than I worry about myself. Some days I even go as far as going into work for him just so he doesn't lose his job.

Today was different. I would not be able to cover for Dad at his work if he couldn't get there. I was going to see Brooks for another session.

I arrived at Brooks's office and immediately got called in for my session. Brooks said to me, "So, Gary, where were we?"

I replied quickly, saying, "Mumbai. We were talking about my escape during the Siege of Mumbai."

Brooks nodded and replied, "Ahh yes. I believe you were driving on quads through the streets the last time we left off. Please continue, Gary, whenever you are ready."

I took a second to gather my thoughts from that chain of events. I found my bearings and continued to tell Brooks my story.

"We were driving through the chaos and madness that were tearing the city apart. We saw ahead of us a high-rise falling down onto the street we were on. This street was our way to the drop off. This street was also our only way to Handmaiden. Seeing the high-rise falling made us crank the accelerator on our quads. We cranked the quad accelerators to get past the falling building before it hit the street. As gravity pulled the building closer and closer to the ground our chances of escape became less and less probable."

Brooks, intrigued as always, asked, "What happened, did you guys make it?"

I thought Brooks was not thinking about what he was asking! If we had not made it, I would not be sitting in his office! I leaned back, crossed my legs, and said, "Well, Brooks, let me tell you how the building crumbled."

⌐ CHAPTER 19 ¬
Collapse

S PEED! SPEED IS WHAT we needed. We needed speed in every facet and in every way. Speed was our only ally. After our quads had reached top speed, we could only hope that we were travelling fast enough. We had to get past that collapsing building before it cut off our escape route. If we were not travelling fast enough to get past that building, we could only hope our deaths would be painless!

As we got closer to the falling high-rise, we were able to see if we were going to live to talk about this race. The probability of our living seemed to get fainter as we felt the wind in our faces from the air being displaced as the high-rise fell. To make sure that I would make it, Saksham looked back at me and screamed, "Lose the backpack!!"

I complied immediately. Complying was my job. Keeping me safe was Saksham's job. Saksham was my handler. I threw my backpack off the quad. I could feel the quad beneath me go slightly faster. I could see myself being able to make it. I could feel the comfort of home already.

As we were driving under the high-rise, it began its final fall onto the ground. Debris was falling all around us. The light we had seen on the other side of the building was getting dimmer. The building was starting to fall on top of us.

We could taste victory in our battle to get past the building when disaster struck. My quad's left front tire blew flat with a resounding bang. My left front tire going flat pulled my quad right into Saksham's quad. When Saksham and I met, we crashed quite unceremoniously.

Out of the corner of my eye, I saw Borris crash as well. He was probably rubbernecking to see how serious the collision between Saksham and I was.

We really did not have time to assess our wounds. We all knew we had to run or be buried alive. We immediately started sprinting towards the exit without a word. I never did understand how we were able to sprint like that. I guess a good dose of adrenalin will enable you to do things that otherwise would be impossible. Each time my feet touched the ground, my hopes of getting home grew weaker.

The high-rise hit the ground, causing dust, debris, and the three of us to be blown everywhere. I was blown at least ten feet from the high-rise. I landed on my stomach and face. I was dazed from the landing but quickly recovered. I sat up and looked to my right. I saw Borris crawling out from under a pile of debris. He looked like he had seen better days!

Borris had blood running from his head and shoulders. A piece of rebar was sticking out of his forearm. When he got out from under the debris, he stood up and walked away from what had been the building. I was pretty sure I saw him spit out a piece of concrete.

I looked around for Saksham. I couldn't see him. I did happen to see was what looked to be a flash drive with the name 'K. Yung' on it. Borris saw the flash drive too and immediately picked it up. He shot me a glance and ordered, "Come on. Let's go."

I pleaded with Borris, "What about Saksham? We can't just leave him behind!"

Without any emotion, Borris responded, "Saksham is dead, Foltz. He didn't make it. We have to get out of here."

I followed Borris through the streets of Mumbai. We dodged patrols and gunfights. We also had to evade massive, dangerous crowds of civilians desperately trying to escape the city. The crowds were dangerous because they had succumbed to mob mentality. Mob mentality is to kill or be killed, and the crowds move in unison.

After Borris and I avoided every patrol, gunfight, and crowd, he brought me to a suburban house. The house seemed to be untouched from the battle. Borris knocked on the door and a voice from the other side cryptically said, "Winter."

Borris, equally cryptically, replied, "Collapse." The door opened. We saw two men. One had opened the door and the other held an assault rifle in his hands. For the 'tough' look, the second man had a cigarette dangling in his mouth. The man holding the door said, "They are waiting for you in the basement."

I hoped that either Handmaiden or a warm bed was waiting. However, the phrase 'they are waiting' made me mentally disqualify the warm bed. Borris and I went down-stairs, ready for some rest and first aid. Borris clearly needed the first aid more than me. When we got downstairs, I saw about four people standing around a table looking at what seemed to be a map. My heart jumped for joy when I noticed one of them was Handmaiden. I wanted so badly to go and say hello, but I was quite forcefully directed over to their medic.

Their medic did some tests on me. He told me that I had a concussion and I needed some rest. I realized that both Handmaiden and the bed were waiting! I complied. I didn't even remember my head hitting the pillow. When I woke up, I felt rejuvenated. I looked around and saw Handmaiden sitting on a chair looking at a map. I got up and approached her. I asked, "So, what's the plan?"

Without missing a beat, she answered, "Get out of the city, make our way to Kabul to help the rebels there for a few days. We will then go straight to Kristiansand, in southern Norway, and cross the North Sea to England. Foltz, I forewarn you, this will not be easy. When we leave Kabul, staying alive will be more difficult than you can possibly imagine."

Handmaiden's warning confused me, so I asked her, "Why is it going to be even more difficult after Kabul?"

Handmaiden briefly looked up at me with surprise on her face. I think she thought I would 'just know." She spread the map out to show me the proposed route to get from Mumbai to Kristiansand and explained, "Alright, Foltz, here is the plan. We leave the city tonight and make our way to Kabul. It is imperative that we keep a low profile, so we will be on foot."

I was quite surprised by this. Travelling on foot worried me because my body wasn't in the best shape. In light of my concern, I asked Handmaiden, "When do we need to be in Kabul?"

Handmaiden got up and walked over to a bench that had a rucksack on it. She picked the rucksack up and motioned to hand it to me. When I grabbed for the rucksack, it almost fell through my fingers. Taking into consideration how easily Handmaiden had picked it up, I was completely unprepared with how heavy the sack was! I had just gained a whole new respect for her physical strength.

Handmaiden looked at me with concern and asked, "Are you sure you can carry that for the next few months? That rucksack is yours until we get to England!"

I slung it over my shoulder and replied lightheartedly, "Yeah, I can manage." I knew that carrying the rucksack would be a serious struggle for the next few months. I decided to accept right then that I could very well die from exhaustion in the next few days.

An intimidating soldier who had been eavesdropping on our conversation butted in, saying, "Alright. I heard what you told Handmaiden. Personally, I think you answered her as you did to try to impress her. Handmaiden is not impressed by words; she is impressed with performance. We both expect you to keep up. SEALs travel at a brisk pace."

I was more than slightly confused. I turned to Handmaiden and asked, "Sorry, who is he? Did I miss something?"

She immediately introduced us. "Foltz, this is Ryan. Ryan is the squad leader of the Navy SEAL team. I have been working with Ryan and his team for the past three months."

Ryan immediately stuck out his right hand and said, "Sorry about my manners. My job is to get all my men home safely.

My job requires me to make sure my men know exactly what is expected of them. Sometimes, depending on the situation, I have to be hard and blunt. This mission is one of those times when I cannot be hard enough or blunt enough. I don't really like it, but I would rather be hard and blunt than having to make room for a body bag." He nodded towards Handmaiden and continued, "Like she said, my name is Ryan. She and I have been working together for the past three months. But my team and I have been in the field for the past two years."

I shook his hand and replied, "That's quite a long time to be in the field. How many casualties have you had, if you don't mind me asking?"

Ryan answered, almost devoid of emotion, "Oh no, not at all. Fair question. In our two years of field time, I have lost four men. We are now twelve strong, including myself. I do sometimes wonder if those four men would still be with us if I had been even tougher on them than I was. My other men tell me that their deaths could not have been avoided. Still a good leader's worst critic is himself. I am definitely no exception to being my own worst critic."

I was actually impressed that Ryan was able to completely control his display of emotion. I knew that being able to control emotional display is key to being an effective leader. Being able to control the display is NOT the same as not having the emotion. A true leader has to be able to lead in spite of circumstances.

Subordinates sometimes confuse the ability to control emotional display with not having emotion. The subordinate sometimes criticizes their leader for the lack of emotional display. Suppressing emotional display is just one of the prices that true leaders have to pay to make sure everyone goes home.

I know when I lost squad mates, I definitely at least batted an eye. But then, I have always known that I am more of a fighter than a leader. Ryan seemed as though he had successfully transformed himself to appear robotic and completely numb to human emotion.

"Glad you two hit it off so well," Handmaiden said with obvious sarcasm and a smirk on her face. "Anyways, we should start getting ready to leave. Ryan, have your guys scout the road ahead for twenty blocks." Handmaiden then pressed her finger on her earpiece and said, "Reggie, join the SEALs scout team as backup. Brian, set this place to blow, and, Zoodle, inform the Mandela that we have the package and we are preparing to leave."

I could only assume that Reggie, Brian, and Zoodle were members of Handmaiden's team and she was giving them their assignments. Since I had 'handlers,' I also assumed that I was 'the package.' Using the phrase 'the Mandela' insinuated either a plane or a ship. I would soon find out that the 'Mandela' was an aircraft carrier named after Nelson Mandela.

The next few hours were spent on careful and precise trip preparation. We needed that time to enable us to leave Mumbai without anyone knowing we were ever there. Most of the preparation was 'need to know.' There were a lot of preparations I didn't see, planned by Ryan and Handmaiden. What I did see was Borris briefing me on the contents of my rucksack. I needed to know how each item worked. There were commonplace items that really did not need much explanation, like the rain poncho, the compass, and the map. There were also a few items I didn't recognize, and I could not even hazard a guess what they were for. Being away from the action really kept me away from the technological advancements.

As Borris and I were finishing packing our rucksacks, I attempted to spark some conversation. "So Borris, what is your next step after we get to England?"

Borris looked at me, concerned, and questioned, "What do you mean? I am not going to England!"

I was confused, so I replied, "What do you mean? You are my handler. You are supposed to make sure I get home… right?"

Borris stopped packing, looked at me, and said, "She didn't tell you, did she?"

"What do you mean she didn't tell me?" I asked incredulously.

Borris explained, "After Kabul, the SEALs and I are splitting off from the group and heading to China. Handmaiden and her team will be taking you the rest of the way to England."

I was a bit sad that Borris and I had to go different ways. But life happens, roll with it. Everyone takes orders from the chain of command. Orders from the chain of command to abandon my friends and me to almost die in Princeton; orders that got my friends and me captured; orders that have given me a chance to escape. Well, nobody's perfect.

⌐ CHAPTER 20 ¬
Stoppage

T HE TIME WAS NOW well after midnight. The only thing that was lighting up the sky was the battle raging on in downtown Mumbai. We moved quickly and quietly through the suburbs. Our movements reminded me of cats in the night. No one saw us or heard us. Whenever we saw someone who wasn't part of our band of eighteen we stopped dead in our tracks and let our camouflage clothing do its job. If someone were trying to find us, they would have to know exactly where we were and how many of us there were.

Escaping Mumbai was actually the least of our worries. What we were most focussed on was the journey ahead through the deserts of Thar and Registan. Handmaiden had mentioned that we could go around the deserts, but going around them would take twice as long due to the EPC Forces we would run into. If we were to go through the deserts, we would completely avoid the EPC, and we would also save time and ammunition. So, we followed her plan and cut through the deserts to fight the battle of attrition instead.

The battle of attrition that we were going to fight is a tricky one. In our battle, we would be fighting the elements. Obviously you can't fight the elements in the traditional sense. Nevertheless, the potential for the elements to thin out your personnel is very real.

In my mind, while I understood Handmaiden's tactics, I questioned if the ends justified the means. We had only a limited amount of water in containers in our rucksacks. The sun was bearing down mercilessly on us. After a little while under that sun, the water would only be wet rather than cool and refreshing.

Each day, we walked deeper into the deserts. I began to think that when, or even if, we got to Kabul, we would be too exhausted to fight! Our situational hazards were those for which the leader must have planned. Handmaiden had it planned out so we wouldn't die from dehydration. Her plan was to go from water to water, or from village to village. While none of us knew that the EPC were using some of the villages as outposts, I just thought it made sense that they would. I was actually kind of disappointed that this seemingly obvious EPC strategy had eluded Handmaiden. We had to improvise.

Handmaiden touched her earpiece and said, "Reggie, what do you see?"

Reggie was lying prone on top of the hill adjacent to us. He was using binoculars. He answered, "It seems to be that the EPC are using this village as an outpost."

Handmaiden looked back at us. She gave each of us a visual scan and asked Reggie, "How many uniforms do you see and how well equipped are they?"

Reggie answered, "I count about a dozen maybe two dozen soldiers, all equipped with older machine guns."

"Any heavy artillery?" asked Handmaiden.

Reggie paused briefly, and then replied, "They have two mounted machine guns in the village. One is mounted on a sandbag pile on the east side. The other is mounted in a mud hut on the west side. They have a mortar pit on the north side. The mortar pit has a watchtower twenty metres to its east. What's the call, boss?"

Handmaiden was weighing her options. To be honest, I did not think she had many options. But then again, identifying options was her job as leader. I was beginning to think that she was going to say something like, "Okay, I have a plan, but you guys aren't going to like it!"

We all waited for Handmaiden's orders to overcome EPC's strategy. We could go to the next village. We would have to hope that the next village did not also have an EPC outpost. The unknown is always a formidable foe! The other main objection to going to the next village was that we would run out of water well before we got there. So, if Handmaiden decided going to the next village was best, somehow we had to get water from this village. She just had to tell us her plan.

Apparently, Handmaiden was having a struggle coming up with a plan. She waved Ryan and a few other SEALs over to her position to talk in private. They talked for a few minutes while the rest of us waited. When they broke their sidebar, Handmaiden talked to the rest of us, saying, "Ok, this is what we are going to do." Everyone, except Borris, listened to her intently. Borris just rolled his eyes at Handmaiden and the other officers.

Handmaiden continued, "We are going to break up into five teams, including backup. Gary, Borris, and Brian, you are with me. Reggie and Zoodle will be backup. SEALs, break yourselves into three teams of four." The SEALs instantly split themselves into three teams of four like they had gone through that exercise hundreds of times. And I thought my team was an organized military unit. These SEALs just made us look like unruly children on a playground.

Once everyone got sorted, Handmaiden explained how we were going to take over the village, "We wait for sundown. We will use the cover of darkness to begin the assault on the village. When Reggie gives us his signal, we split off in four different directions. Eddie's team will attack from the left side. My team will attack from left side middle. Ryan's team will attack from right side middle. Dumaine's team will attack from the right side. Eddie and Dumaine, your paths have the machine gun nests. Your teams MUST stay hidden from view from the nests. Let's take this village quickly and cleanly. Any questions? Good. We attack at sundown."

We were sitting together in our teams, waiting for sundown. It was taking forever, so I attempted to spark up a conversation with my team. "Hey Brian, how long have you been in the field?"

Brian was of average height but built like a truck. I could tell he had been in Delta Force for quite some time. He was a bit older, and he always had his rifle in his hands at the ready. Brian was always keenly aware of his surroundings. He wore a clerical collar, which indicated he was probably some sort of field chaplain.

He looked over at me and replied, "Seventeen years." Then he inquired, "Why do you ask?"

I was slightly surprised that he even replied, so he caught me off guard a bit, but I quickly responded. "No, I don't mean how long you have been in the military. I mean how long have you been in the field? Ryan told me that he and his SEAL team have been in the field for two years. As for myself, I have been in the field for ten years, if you don't include my time in the hospital after Princeton."

Something about my time in hospital confused Brian. He looked at me with a confused scowl. I really could not discern what I had said that could confuse him. I was just about to ask him if I had said something wrong when he asked for clarification. "What do you mean, *after* Princeton?"

I began to explain to him what happened during my time in Princeton. I described hearing blood-curdling screams. I talked about the horror of seeing human beings being mercilessly ripped apart by different types of weapons. I even graphically recalled soldiers being so hungry that they resorted to cannibalism. I didn't spare one detail. I was amazed that after all that effort to get a response from Brian, he didn't so much as flinch. If what I saw and went through in Princeton didn't faze Brian, I can only imagine what he had seen.

"Guys, it's almost sundown. Start getting ready," ordered Handmaiden. Immediately, everyone complied. We all picked up our gear and started climbing up the hill. Our military training showed as we climbed in a straight line within our designated groups.

I was right behind Brian. Borris was behind me. Handmaiden was at the front of the line leading us in the assault. We were about to get to the top of the hill when Handmaiden suddenly stopped and put her fist up to signal 'all stop.' The rest of us stopped as a unit. Handmaiden put her fist down and cautioned, "There is still sunlight between us and the village." Then she ordered, "Wait for my signal."

We waited, physically still but mentally on edge, for her signal. After what seemed an eternity, Handmaiden motioned her arm forward rapidly. We all took off as quickly and quietly as possible. We wanted to accomplish our objective cleanly. Everyone was at full sprint to get across the field without being seen. About halfway through the field we began to fan out into our groups, as ordered. Just as my group got to the first building we had to clear, the EPC shot a flare into the air. It lit up the sky. We were completely exposed. The flare had completely removed our advantage of darkness.

The thought did occur to me that the flare was nothing more than the EPC doing a routine test. The absence of excited EPC soldier voices seemed to bear this out. We just had to stay quiet.

Unfortunately, I was being far too optimistic. All of the planning that Ryan, Handmaiden, and the others had done was unravelling so fast, not even time was able to keep up with the events that followed.

After the flare, the EPC fired their machine guns. The bullets were flying everywhere. When the EPC ran out of bullets, they fired their heavy-duty mortars. The mortar bombardment caused the ground to shake. Soon the bodies started to pile up. After thirty minutes of insane fighting, the village looked more like a tomb than anywhere people had lived."

Brooks looked at me and asked, "If you don't mind, Gary, can you please try and explain to me what happened during the incursion?"

I hesitated to reply and said, "It all went by so fast, I can't even explain it. One moment, there is no sound anywhere, and the next moment, the whole village is lit up like a Christmas tree with guns firing and soldiers dying."

Brooks leaned forward and said, "Try and slow it down, Gary. Breathe slowly and focus on the moment."

I sarcastically replied, "Well, Brooks, I would love to tell you but I was knocked unconscious when the flare lit up the sky. Everything I have told you was actually what I was told by other survivors."

Brooks gave me a glare of acceptance… but acceptance to what, I wondered?

⌐ CHAPTER 21 ¬
Bested by a Monkey

ROOKS WAS STRONGLY PACING back and forth around the room. His left forearm was crossed over his torso. His right upper arm was resting on his left wrist. His right forearm was holding his right hand up over his mouth. The look on his face was that of someone trying to remember something. I was intrigued. I was very much anticipating what he remembered, whatever it may be. I welcomed any discussion that would help me recover from my past traumas.

Brooks came to a stop. I could see in his face that he had mentally found the memory, which was the reason to carry on with the appointment. "Ok, Gary, I am not sure why you don't remember the attack. The mental trauma your brain experienced during the attack may have been too severe. Or it could be from something that hit your head. Who knows, but let's just continue from what you remember after the attack."

I replied, "Well, I felt as though I had just awakened from a dream."

Brooks, glad that I had at least remembered *some*thing, said, "Good! Now, please continue."

I paused to recollect my past memories and continued. "I was leaning up against a wall. Handmaiden was shaking my shoulders to wake me up. At least, that is the first thing I remember after the battle."

"Gary. Gary! GARY!!" Handmaiden yelled.

I didn't know how I got to that wall, and that frightened me. I had no recollection of the battle. I shook my head to get rid of the mental cobwebs. My squad mates must have dragged me from the village outskirts to the wall. I was very confused.

I scanned my surroundings. I saw an elderly woman in the village sweeping her front doorstep to my right. I also saw one of the SEALs carrying four bloodied and damaged dog tags. His head and posture were slumped, as one would when mourning. Our whole team had suffered casualties during the attack. SEALs are supposed to be the best-trained fighters in the world, but even the best of the best cannot avoid casualties in combat.

Handmaiden snapped her fingers in front of my face to get my attention. Again she yelled at me, "Gary! You are hurt! How bad is it? Wake up and look at me!"

I quickly looked at myself from head to toe and only saw minor cuts and bruises. I looked back at Handmaiden and groggily replied, "What happened? How did I get here? Just flesh wounds."

Handmaiden replied, "Well, from my perspective, a building beside us exploded. The explosion knocked you unconscious. We dragged you over here and tried to make you look as dead as possible. We kicked some dirt on you and took your dog tags." Handmaiden paused, reached into her vest, pulled out my dog tags, handed them to me, and said, "And here they are." With a smirk, she added, "Try not to lose them again!"

I was still shaken from the blast. Coming to terms with Handmaiden's explanation was considerably difficult. I guess that's what happens when you suffer a concussion, but, then again, that was just my best guess. From what I could discern, I was unconscious for only about an hour.

Inside the village, remnants of destroyed houses were burning. Just outside the village, a pile of corpses was burning – the only sources of light in the entire area.

Then I remembered why we were there. I asked Handmaiden, "Is the water well intact?"

Before she could answer, Borris interrupted us and answered, "Don't worry about the well, Gary, we have secured it." He smiled and handed me a full canteen.

Being very dehydrated, I grabbed the canteen from him like an animal and drained it down my parched throat. The cool, wet, water felt SO good going down!

"Do you feel better?" asked Handmaiden.

I took a second to gather myself from chugging down almost a whole litre of water. My stomach began to twist and turn. I knew I was going to vomit. There was nothing I could do to stop it. I struggled to my feet and ran/limped around the corner. I leaned against the wall and let my body do the rest. I just did not want Handmaiden or Borris to see me losing control like that. I knew that they were well aware of what I was doing, but they initially afforded me the dignity of losing control in private.

Handmaiden and Borris slowly followed me and watched me puke my guts out. I could hear them chuckling and making jokes behind me. After I vomited, I walked back to them. As I was approaching, Borris smirked and said to me, "Hey Foltz, here's a tip… if you are dehydrated like you were, don't chug a whole litre of water like that. It will make you puke your guts out."

I knew Borris was just having fun with me, so I replied in kind, "Thanks, Borris, I will keep that in mind."

Borris, still with the smirk on his face, added, "No problem, if you need any tips on surviving in the great outdoors just ask me; it is what I am trained to do."

Borris's statement saying that he was trained to survive in the wild piqued my curiosity. I asked him, "What do you mean, 'it is what I am trained to do'?" I wanted to know if he was just talking big or if he had actually trained in outdoor survival.

Borris lost the smirk and explained, "Well, back in the day, when I was in government special forces, I was the survival specialist. I was trained to guide teams through uncharted territories."

Handmaiden looked at him with confused anger. With attitude, she confronted him, demanding, "Why didn't you tell me this before? Ryan and I could have put your skills to work. I am NOT pleased that you hid skills from us that you knew would be useful. Explain yourself! Explain why you didn't tell us back in Mumbai!!"

Without missing a beat, Borris calmly replied, "I watched what you were doing. You did what I would have done. I reasoned that I did not need to intervene. Anyways, the safety of the VIP comes before anything else, and he was safe."

Borris's calm demeanor infuriated Handmaiden. She grabbed Borris, pinned him against the wall, pulled out her sidearm, and planted it against his temple. He didn't even try to defend himself. He let her throw him around like a rag doll.

Before Handmaiden could say anything, Borris, calm as ever, said, "Trust me, you don't want to do this."

Handmaiden was angrier than I had ever seen her. She was actually scaring me. I had witnessed her feats of strength and her ability to remain calm under extreme pressure. I could not blame her for losing her cool, given the circumstance. I did think that Borris was purposely pushing her buttons, but I did not understand why. With fire in her eyes, Handmaiden pushed her gun harder into his temple and hissed at him, "Yeah? Tell me why I shouldn't want to do this?"

Borris simply answered, "'Cause your safety is on." His voice was annoyingly poised. I guessed Handmaiden did not scare him. I could not even begin to hazard a guess why.

Being told that her safety was on was apparently the last thing that Handmaiden expected Borris to say. For a split second, she looked at her gun. That split second that she took to check her safety was all the time Borris needed to disarm her and reverse the past situation.

Now Handmaiden was pinned against the wall and Borris was pushing Handmaiden's own pistol into her forehead. He gave her a long, hard stare. Borris wanted to make sure that Handmaiden clearly understood that he was not to be messed with.

I watched them both as Handmaiden's squad mates and the SEALs began to gather around. They were screaming at Borris to let her go. They screamed that if he did not let her go, they would shoot him dead. Borris did not flinch. He did not even acknowledge that he was being screamed at. Handmaiden was beginning to panic because she was trying to escape Borris, and he was just too strong. As she panicked, Borris began to lift her with one hand, by her neck, while his other hand was still pressing the gun to her temple.

I could see that Handmaiden was frightened and embarrassed because a lowly bodyguard was overpowering her. She was kicking and yelling at Borris to put her down. Borris just kept his vice-like grip on her neck, being very careful not to choke Handmaiden. Borris seemed to have no intention of letting her go.

With all her remaining strength, Handmaiden pulled out her combat knife and tried to stab Borris's arm. Before she could do any damage, Borris unceremoniously dropped her to the ground. To add insult to injury, he shot three times around Handmaiden's head. No one expected the shots, and Handmaiden froze. Her knife slipped through her fingers and fell to the ground. Borris turned Handmaiden's handgun safety back on and laid it on the ground gently at her feet and calmly said, "That's why."

Borris turned around to face the audience of SEALs and Delta Force operatives. Borris's audience was in complete shock from what they had just seen. The SEALs and operatives really did not know what to expect from him next. With absolute confidence in his abilities, Borris casually walked through them, over to the elderly lady's hut, laid on her door-step, and went to sleep.

Barely able to fully comprehend my story, Brooks summed up his reaction with, "So, you're telling me that a person, whom everybody thought was nothing but a run-of-the-mill bodyguard, physically bested a top-tier Delta Force operative, mentally beat the other thirteen Special Forces operatives, AND stymied the SEALs. And he did all of that without saying a word."

I chuckled and replied, "Well, there is a saying that actions speak louder than words. Actually, my recount of what happened is pretty lame compared to having seen it firsthand!"

Brooks was riveted with my story. He was leaning forward, sitting, literally, on the edge of his seat, with his eyes wide, waiting for me to continue. "Well, what happened next?"

With a smirk, I said, "Well, to the best of my knowledge, nobody ever so much as hinted at a challenge with Borris again."

Brooks was confused, but just for a second, and asked, "What do you mean, 'to the best of my knowledge?'"

Sarcastically, I answered, "Aren't you paying attention to the story, Brooks? Remember the plan that Borris told me. We were to part ways after Kabul, and that's what we did."

Brooks got a little defensive and retorted, "Of course I'm paying attention! I just got caught up in your story, that's all. Anyways, continue."

I replied, "Well, the morning after Borris' and Handmaiden's showdown, we got up at dawn and began our very long hike to Kabul."

┌ CHAPTER 22 ┐
A Hike and a Half

ACH DAY'S GOAL WAS merely survival. Survival in a desert is always a gamble – the gamble being whether or not you will unintentionally do the one thing that causes your death. Truth be told, when you are in a desert, you always feel like you are dying, and your body never stops quietly screaming for relief.

Different parts of us were making their own protests. Our mouths were so dry, our spit looked like chalk. Our legs were numb from pushing our feet through the sand. Our skin was beet red from the sun beating down on us mercilessly. Some locals took pity on us and gave us some lotion to take the edge off our agony.

Handmaiden and Ryan were making full use of their new knowledge of Borris's survival expertise. We would not have made it on time, nor in the shape we did, without Borris. He guided us from the first water stop all the way to Kabul. I have never really been able to figure out exactly how he got us to Kabul. That riddle almost blows my mind, let alone the added fact that he got us into Kabul undetected. I just had to stop thinking about getting into Kabul undetected!

Borris signalled us to stop by sticking his fist up. Handmaiden very carefully approached him and quietly whispered, "What seems to be the problem?"

Borris replied in a whisper, "The EPC is watching who enters the city. We can't go into Kabul like this. We will be shot on sight. We must be strategic. We must go underground." Borris, knowing full well that our objective was in Kabul, turned around and began to walk away from the city.

Handmaiden immediately grabbed Borris's arm and objected to his leading us away from the city. She pointed out the obvious by saying, "Borris, we aren't moles! With our manpower and resources, we can't dig a tunnel and still meet our objective."

Borris looked back at her and said, "You are correct, but I know someone who can."

After hearing Borris's assurance that he 'knew a guy,' we fell in behind him. We followed him without question for the next few hours. Borris brought us to a townhouse just outside the Kabul outskirts. It seemed very normal for Borris's taste. Maybe the townhouse seemed *too* normal for Borris's taste.

Borris approached the front door of the townhouse. He turned his head and cautioned us, "Don't say a word. I will do the talking."

As obedient as ever, we all complied with Borris's instruction. We proceeded to communicate with hand signals.

Handmaiden told the SEALs to take a look around the house. She told me to stay close to her. I did not see anyone signalling concern.

Borris knocked on the door. An old man opened the door with a big smile. As soon as he saw Borris, his whole countenance completely changed from one of welcoming to absolute rejection. The old man spoke with Borris in a language foreign to me. I was quite surprised when Borris responded to him fluently. It seemed like they were close friends. We were all getting impatient because we needed to get inside and out of sight before the old man got caught talking to outsiders, especially ones with the equipment and weapons we had.

Ryan spoke to Handmaiden as carefully as he could. "Handmaiden, we've got an EPC convoy coming our way."

Handmaiden needed information about the convoy. "How are they armed?"

Ryan answered, "A couple of trucks with turrets on them, and at least one APC."

Handmaiden turned toward Borris and sternly informed him, "Borris, hurry it up! A convoy is coming our way and we aren't equipped to fight it."

The old man then looked towards Handmaiden but asked Borris, "Wait! Are you guys running from EPC?"

We all nodded at him in panic. We were wondering if he would let us in or not. If the old man did let us in, he would help us dodge another bullet. Just another bullet on this roller coaster of an adventure my former squad mates would have called 'a mission.'

The old man hastily invited us in, waving his hand inward. "Come in, come in! Hurry up, come in."

All fourteen of us attempted to rush into the townhouse, which was too small. We could not all fit without getting caught. In our panic, Borris had remained calm. He had walked down the hallway and found a bedroom. Borris signalled us into the bedroom and asked for help. "Help me move the bed." Once again, Borris had saved our skins.

Ryan and some of his SEALs helped lift the bed. Lifting the bed exposed a trap door. Handmaiden opened the trap door. She was about to go down the stairs, but Borris stopped her.

"What are you doing, Borris?" Handmaiden demanded quietly, in anger.

"Let me go first. I know the way," said Borris.

Borris's logic made sense, so Handmaiden stepped out of the way for Borris. He began his descent down the ladder, with Handmaiden right behind him. Handmaiden's squad mates followed her. The SEALs and I followed her squad mates.

When I got down to the bottom of the ladder, I looked around very briefly. There appeared to be only the one tunnel going in one direction.

We later found out that there was a whole network of underground tunnels going all across the Middle East. Some of the tunnels stretched as far east as the Chinese western borders, and other tunnels snaked into southern Russia. These were used to secretly move resistance fighters, food, weapons, and ammunition from point A to point B. Since the resistance fighters were on our side, we used the tunnels. The RUD are probably still using them to move assets around the Middle East.

Brooks's facial expression changed. He now looked at me with concern and mild confusion. He opened his mouth slightly like he was going to ask me a question, but changed his mind. Brooks not saying anything really confused me. I asked, "Brooks, it seemed like you were going to ask me something, but the look on your face made me think you just changed your mind."

Brooks' eyes began to nervously jump from side to side. I strongly suspect that he was trying to hide something from me. I called him on my suspicion and asked, "Brooks, what are you not telling me?"

Brooks replied immediately. "Oh, don't worry about it. It's nothing. Please continue your story. You were going through underground tunnels to get into Kabul."

Brooks' answer only made my suspicions grow that he was not being forthright. Something was going on with Brooks. There was something that he did not want to admit to. I would look into it on my own time. For the moment, I'd continue with the session. I continued my story about the underground tunnels. "Yes, we were going through underground tunnels to get to Kabul."

"And how long did it take you to get to the city?" asked Brooks.

I took a second to gather my thoughts and continued my story. "About a day, I think. I am not too sure. When we went down into the tunnels, it was well after dark. When we got back up from the tunnels, we found ourselves in midday. While we had a pretty good idea that we had not been in the tunnels for more than a day, we had no way of knowing for sure."

Brooks's office door opened and his assistant poked her head in, saying, "Brooks, Mr. Lennox is ready to see you now."

"Okay, thanks, Betty. I'm sorry to cut you off there, Gary, but we are out of time and my next client is ready. Same time next week, right?" questioned Brooks, looking to me for confirmation.

I empathized with Brooks. "Don't worry about cutting me off, Brooks. I told you a lot today that I haven't told anyone else. Yes, I'll see you next week."

Brooks and I shook hands. I began to make my exit when I crossed paths with Mr. Lennox. He looked like every other army vet I had seen before. Army vets look rough and tough, but their eyes show a lot of sadness. Their eyes say that their emotional state is very tenuous. I was very much in the same situation.

Then I realized that Brooks didn't look the same as all the other vets. His eyes just did not have that sadness, and that really grabbed my curiosity. Brooks appeared aloof. He certainly did not seem to be on the brink of collapse.

That night I tried to do some research on Brooks. I wanted to figure out who my therapist was and how he had changed during his time in the war. I typed 'Brooks' into the search bar, and I found out just how common the 'Brooks' surname was. There were thousands of 'Brooks.' So I searched my memories of him talking about himself, and I added those details into the filter. I added that Brooks had been a soldier. He had been tortured. Brooks had also possibly fought in Egypt when it was invaded in 2056.

My search engine yielded no results. I checked again and again. I was beginning to think Brooks wasn't his real name, or that his record got completely redacted. The search results insinuated that he didn't even exist!

I was more than a little perturbed. The search results insinuated that my therapist's true identity could be anything. Brooks could be a politician in hiding. He could also be an undercover handler keeping a close eye on me. I needed answers from Brooks. Every passing day brought a new level of anxiety into my life. Unfortunately, there was absolutely nothing I could do about my predicament! I could only wait until my next appointment with Brooks.

⌐ CHAPTER 23 ¬
The Dirt Behind a Clean Slate

WALKED INTO BROOKS'S RECEPTION area quite abruptly. I wanted him to come clean, and I wanted him to come clean NOW! When the receptionist saw me, she knew better than to try to have me take a seat. She immediately led me into Brooks's office. I proceeded in cautiously. I saw him standing at his window looking out into the city. He had a glass of booze in his hand. Brooks turned around. He had a slight smirk on his face. He greeted me, saying, "Gary, it's nice to see you. How has life been for you this past week?"

He seemed more polite than usual. He was not acting like the Brooks I knew. There was just something about him that was unfamiliar. The look on his face told me he knew what I found out about him and his past. Brooks also knew that he had to very subtly distract me so he would not have to explain what I had learned.

I had never seen Brooks drink in his office. Maybe he hid it and only partook for special occasions. If Brooks did drink only for special occasions, how was this day special for him? And how did I fit in? I decided to act as I normally do to try to throw him off his plan.

I replied, "Life has been treating me well, Brooks." Pointing out his drink, I continued, "You seem to have something to celebrate. What's the occasion?"

Brooks looked down at his glass and replied with a chuckle. "Oh, I was saving this scotch for when the war ended. The war was supposed to end ten years ago. I am drinking it now just because I can." He offered, "Want some?"

I replied with a small amount of defensiveness. "No, thanks. I am good. After what happened to me at the Mumbai festival, I don't touch the stuff anymore."

Brooks nodded and replied, "Well, Gary, I can't argue with that." He motioned to a chair and continued, "Please, have a seat. Get comfortable."

I sat down to start our session. I mentally filed in the back of my mind the fact that Brooks wasn't who he said he was.

He sat down, calmly held his drink in his hand, and said, "So, where did we leave off?"

I glared at Brooks. I knew that if I didn't come right out and ask him about what I had learned, I would never again have the nerve to ask. I needed a small distraction, so I tried to peel the Band-Aid off my hand. At the same time, I decided to use Brooks's intoxication to my advantage. I got right to the point. "Brooks, what did you do before becoming a therapist?"

Brooks looked at me in the same manner that the guards in Mongolia had looked at me. His facial expression, intentional or otherwise, insinuated that he was all-knowing and in control. Even though Brooks was under the influence of alcohol, the situation made me feel as though he controlled everything in the room. I mentally prepared myself for the conversation he and I were about to have. I anticipated that the conversation was going to be even more difficult than I had imagined!

In an attempt to stall for time to figure out exactly how he wanted to answer me, Brooks asked me, "Are you sure you want to go down that road, Gary?"

I hesitated to respond. I could play the stalling game too. I began to wonder what I was about to get myself into. I weighed the pros and cons of continuing the conversation. We both had an advantage. Brooks' advantage was his knowledge. My advantage was his intoxication.

I wanted to increase my advantage over Brooks. I wracked my brain for ways I could increase my advantage. The first realistic plan that came to mind was a game of timmeal. So I asked him, "Brooks, would you mind playing a game of timmeal?"

Brooks was definitely not expecting my game invitation. Unfortunately for me, he seemed to recover from his surprise far too quickly. He answered, "I will take your invitation as a 'yes, you do want to go down that road.' I will set the game up." Brooks got up, got the timmeal game out, and began to set it up.

I was nervous. The last time I played this was in college. College was many years ago, but I still thought I could beat him. After all, I had been the reigning college champ when I was there!

Brooks was just about done setting up the game when he stopped. I thought 'now what?' Brooks looked up at me and said, "Before we begin, I want to forewarn you that I am a three-time world champion of this game."

I froze. I struggled to reply. "Excuse me, what did you say?"

Brooks threw his dice down and announced, "Let's begin. We are playing for best of seven!"

Brooks caught me completely off guard. He had taken the strategic advantage! When I played in college, both players had to be ready to roll at the same time. Brooks's style of play was a street fight.

Talk about a momentum shift! I originally thought that I had the upper hand with the game challenge. Then Brooks pulled the rug out from under me with a starting move I did not see coming! I never suspected that Brooks would start the game the way he did. Clearly, Brooks was not bluffing when he said he had won three world titles in this game.

He beat me in quick succession in our first three matches. I was certain that I would lose without so much as getting off the 'start' position. My challenge seemed like it was going down without even a puff of smoke.

Then, once again, the momentum shifted. I began to find my rhythm. I began to steal small victories. I put enough small victories together and I found myself winning a game. Then I won another game. In a whirlwind of strategy, I managed to win three games in a row. Neither Brooks nor I could believe we were playing the seventh and deciding game.

Both of our overlords had taken massive hits. Brooks had lost his bodyguards but I had not. I had the advantage. I was going to win. I was countering his every move. I could see that Brooks was getting frustrated. Imagine that: a three-time world champion being bested by a vet who had not played in years. The onus was on Brooks to make a mind-blowing move.

I was pretty sure I had him where I wanted him. I was going to win. I decided to make a bold move. What did I have to lose? I took charge. I used my bodyguard to take down his overlord... AGAIN! Brooks countered by putting down his last ability card, a wolf thorns card. A wolf thorns card reverses all damage done to the targeted unit by the attacker and doubled.

My bodyguard was now dead. With one move, the three-time world champion had completely turned the tables on me. And it was now Brooks's turn. He was going to win.

Brooks grabbed his overlord piece and commented, "Gary, what I have observed from you during this game has been very eye opening for me. I don't want any bad blood between us. I concede this game. I will tell you who I really am... But first you must finish your story."

I was surprised, elated, and confused. Why would he concede knowing he was going to win? I calmly replied, "Alright, Brooks, where were we?"

┌ CHAPTER 24 ┐
A Taste of Freedom

A S WE LEFT THE underground tunnels, we emerged onto the streets of Kabul. Borris handed each of us a poncho. The poncho had two purposes. It was to help us conceal our gear, and to prevent us from blowing our cover.

Handmaiden's plan was to reach the Resistance and give them the help they needed. Once the Resistance had been helped, our three 'teams' would split up to continue separate missions. The three teams were the Resistance, the SEALs and Borris, and Handmaiden's team and myself. The Resistance would stay the course where they were. The SEALs and Borris were going to China for a top-secret mission. Handmaiden's team was tasked with getting me home safely.

Handmaiden's team, the SEALS, and I started following Borris. After following him through the streets of Kabul for a few minutes, he led us to what resembled a restaurant. We were all confused, but we had absolute confidence in Borris. Like sheep, we willingly followed Borris into the wannabe restaurant. To our surprise, the building actually was a restaurant!

But something about it just didn't feel right. Experienced soldiers develop a gut feeling. My gut feeling was tingling big time! As soon as we were all in the restaurant, a young waitress approached us. She began speaking to Borris. My best guess is that she was speaking Hindi. Once again, Borris surprised the living daylights out of me when he replied right back to her. Again, my best guess is that he was also speaking Hindi.

When the waitress and Borris ended their conversation, she motioned for us to follow her. She led us through the kitchen to a staircase. The staircase led down to the basement. In the basement were six men of various ages. All six men were armed with old machine guns from wars in the early 21st century.

One of the older men, whom I assumed to be their leader, approached us. The man spoke to us in English. "I understand you Americans are our backup."

Borris's face broke into a very small but reassuring smile, and he replied, "Yes. We are your backup."

The leader nodded and explained his plan. "The charges are being set as we speak. Your job is to attack from the rooftops. When the enemy and their drones are neutralized, pillage the cargo trucks. Grab whatever supplies you need. After you secure the supplies you need, you may go as you please. I have been told that you are splitting into two groups. I do not care what your missions are. Neither do I care where you are going. However, we have already put aside trucks, food, water, and clean clothes for you when you return."

Borris approached the leader, shook his hand, and said, "Thank you so much for your help. Our supplies are running low. We will take care of that convoy in no uncertain terms."

Borris turned to us and put us into teams. He told each team where he wanted them. My directive was to stay in the restaurant's basement. I was to wait for Handmaiden, or one of her squad mates, to come and get me. I was not particularly impressed with that decision, but I understood and accepted it because I was the VIP and they had to secure me in the safest manner they could arrange.

Everyone else left to complete their teams' respective assignments. I took a seat on a box of kitchen supplies. I sat there for what seemed like an eternity. I later found out that I only sat there for a few hours. I tried unsuccessfully to make conversation with a young man who didn't know English. Well, that's not exactly true. He did know how to say 'shut up,' but he had no clue what 'shut up' meant. I figured this out because one time I reached for my canteen and he yelled, 'Shut up!!' at me. He used 'shut up' as an answer for everything. I found that amusing. Mentally, I began to refer to him as my babysitter.

After sitting in awkward silence with my babysitter, I heard people coming down the stairs. I looked to the stairs and recognized Zoodle and Reggie.

Reggie looked at me with wild fear in his eyes. With extreme urgency in his voice, he ordered, "Foltz, come with us. We are leaving town NOW!"

Without hesitation I stood up and ran with them to where Zoodle and Reggie had been told the trucks would be hidden. The trucks were originally hidden for when the teams returned from their missions, but emergencies change plans on the fly.

As we ran, I was glad that Zoodle and Reggie knew where the trucks were hidden! We ran with urgency in every step. We ran for blocks. The streets became a blur. We didn't stop for anything. I began to think we were running straight out of the city. I also began to think there could be only one reason for us to run so hard – because our cover had been blown. If our cover had been blown, the EPC would be closing in on us.

We reached an empty alleyway. Reggie raised his fist, signalling for us to stop.

My curiosity finally got the better of me, and I abruptly blurted out, "Hey guys, what's going on?!"

Zoodle and Reggie were both exhausted. They looked at each other hesitantly. Between heavy breaths, Reggie answered me, "This is not what it looks like."

Zoodle continued, "Handmaiden ordered us to meet her at this location. We were supposed to meet her here over an hour ago."

"Alright, so what is her plan for us?" I asked.

Zoodle continued, "We were to secure the convoy, grab you, bring you here, and wait for ten minutes. Handmaiden insisted that we understand that if she doesn't show up, our only focus is to get you home safely. We both assured her that we clearly understood."

I questioned Zoodle and Reggie again about Handmaiden's odd directive. "Well, an ultimate directive like that would seem out of character for Handmaiden. Do you think she suspected an imminent, overwhelming attack? I mean, why else would she insist that you make sure I get home?"

Reggie and Zoodle looked at each other with blank expressions. They clearly did not know what Handmaiden's reasoning was. Reggie looked back at me and lamented, "We have no idea why she would make a call like this."

Just as Reggie finished his lament, a van pulled up at the end of the alley. The van's sliding door opened. I couldn't see who was inside. I did hear someone inside yelling out, "Checkmate!"

Zoodle immediately replied in an excited tone, "Kingfish!" Zoodle turned to Reggie and me. He motioned with his head for us to get in the van, and said, "Guys, this ride is for us."

Reggie and I followed Zoodle to the van. We hopped in. The door closed behind us. We took our seats and rode off into the night.

On the journey home with apparently what was left of Handmaiden's team, it was actually kind of nice to feel like somewhat of a free man again. The closer to home I got, the freer I felt. Despite feeling freer, the fear of getting caught preoccupied my mind. I knew that getting caught would mean an all-expense paid trip back to Mongolia or Mumbai. Unfortunately, there would be no expenses to be paid for that trip! I would rather die than be back in the enemy's custody.

Brooks interjected, "What did it feel like? You know, being on the run from the enemy again? Was it exhilarating? Were you scared? Were you concerned what would happen if you got caught? Maybe they wouldn't even bother bringing you back. Maybe they would just shoot you on the spot."

"That is a very good question, Brooks, but it isn't that easy to answer," I replied.

Brooks's face changed expression and he frowned at me. He asked, "Why is my question hard to answer? Why isn't the answer a 'yes' or 'no'?"

I smiled and replied, "Well, Brooks, I could just say, yes it was scary to always have to look over your shoulder while running behind enemy lines. But when you succeed in escaping, you always have at least a pinch of joy springing up from inside of you. So it's easier to tell you what actually happened rather than try and beat around the bush with yes or no questions."

Brooks wants me to continue with my story, "Well, if that's the case, Gary, tell me what happened after Kabul."

"Let me tell you, what happened after Kabul is a story in itself!" I replied. Brooks's expression changed to one of anticipation...

⌐ CHAPTER 25 ¬
Into the Night

A S WE LEFT KABUL, I could hear the war tearing the city apart. The explosions and artillery fire were so loud we could have easily mistaken the van for a convertible with the top down! The experience made me think of what happened to Mumbai. Kabul was just on a smaller scale.

Handmaiden was driving the van. Zoodle was her navigator. If Zoodle miscommunicated with Handmaiden, we would most certainly be as good as dead! The van could be blown up by artillery fire or EPC soldiers could stop us. If *any*thing unexpected occurred, everyone's efforts to get us this far would have been in vain.

Zoodle and Handmaiden required absolute correct communication. The rest of us had to be dead quiet for Zoodle and Handmaiden to have that correct communication. We knew our very lives depended on quiet. We felt frustrated that, other than being dead quiet, there was absolutely nothing we could do to help Zoodle and Handmaiden. Fortunately, Zoodle and Handmaiden achieved that absolute correct communication! They got us out of Kabul unscathed.

The coming days were harsh. We had to overcome challenges every day. We could not stop for fuel because we had no way to pay. Besides, even if we could pay, the EPC would have taken the opportunity to close in. We knew that when we ran out of fuel, we would have to make the rest of the journey on foot. We ran out of fuel halfway to Dushanbe.

We walked for three days to get to Dushanbe. We secured some horses there, then we rode horseback through Kyrgyzstan to the Kazakhstan border. The horses died at the Kazakhstan border from exhaustion and malnutrition.

Once again, we were on foot, in the winter. We hiked through the Kazakhstani Mountains. We had little food and even less ammunition. We knew that when we ran out of ammunition, we would have to use the enemy weapons we had found on the way. The thought of using enemy weapons did not thrill us because they were old and poorly made.

Brooks could no longer contain his curiosity. He wanted to know what kind of a timeframe I had summarized. He asked, "At this point, Gary, how long had you been on your journey?"

I answered, "We left Mumbai in December of 2061. We had been on our journey for about four months."

"And, psychologically speaking, how did your group handle those four months?" Brooks inquired.

I replied with a hint of brutal frankness, "I didn't mind it. Unfortunately, Zoodle and Reggie were on the brink of collapse."

I continued my story. "The night was young, our stomachs were empty, and we were travelling on adrenalin. I had dealt with these conditions many times before. The others? Not so much."

"'Zoodle, how much further to the next village?' asked Handmaiden.

Zoodle turned to Handmaiden to reply but managed only a mumbled gibberish. We had no idea what he tried to say. The effort to talk, as small as it was, was too much for him. Zoodle collapsed. He began quivering in the snow. Zoodle was dying! If he did die, the rest of us knew we had just been sentenced to death. We would be lost in Kazakhstan. One by one, the elements would kill us all!

We knew we had to do everything we could to keep Zoodle alive. We made a makeshift sled for him to lie on and rest. We did what we could, which wasn't much, to keep him warm. We dragged him across the Tarbagatai Mountains. We did this for five gruelling days. I will never understand how the rest of us survived while dragging him!"

"How *did* the rest of you survive?" asked Brooks.

I continued, speaking candidly, and said, "We were all exhausted. We took turns dragging Zoodle. Even when we weren't dragging Zoodle, we could barely stand. To make matters worse, we were out of food as well."

We knew we were dragging, basically, a dead man across the mountains. Zoodle was extremely weak. He mustered his strength and, with monumental effort, he began to mutter something somewhat coherently. We immediately stopped pulling the sled to concentrate on what he was saying.

When Handmaiden realized that Zoodle was desperately trying to talk, she ran back to the sled. Handmaiden tried to gently appeal to Zoodle's will to survive. "Zoodle. It's me. Handmaiden. Stay awake. Zoodle! Stay with us. We *are* getting help!"

Zoodle wearily groaned and replied, "What? Who is Zoodle?" He looked up at Handmaiden, very confused, and asked, "And Emma, why are you calling yourself Handmaiden?"

Zoodle then passed out. The colour of his face told us he was struggling to stay alive. But he had done two things that piqued my curiosity. He had asked who 'Zoodle' was, AND he had called Handmaiden 'Emma.' I had so many questions racing through my head, but they would have to wait. There would be a more appropriate time to get answers.

"Hey guys, look!" Reggie was excitedly pointing to the north. He could hardly contain his enthusiasm. He continued, "There's smoke coming from over there."

We all looked towards him and followed his hand to where he was pointing. Truth be told, we all thought Reggie was hallucinating. Imagine our surprise when we realized that there *was* smoke coming from the north.

I looked to Handmaiden and said, "Boss, what's the call?"

Handmaiden looked at Zoodle, then towards the smoke. I could see she was mentally juggling the pros and cons of what her next decision would entail. The strained look on her face convinced me that she was also having trouble separating true pros and cons from those of possible hallucination. I stepped in to give her brain a chance to regain her objectivity. I approached her but turned my head to Brian and volunteered, "Hey, Brian, hang back on this one. I can handle this."

Handmaiden nodded her agreement to Brian. He needed someone new to brainstorm with because he had also sensed that Handmaiden needed a break. I went over to Brian, who appreciated that I would have a different perspective. We both felt a rush of newfound energy. We brainstormed and came up with a plan.

Brian and I broke our huddle and faced the rest, side by side, as co-leaders. Brian began telling everyone the plan. "Alright, here is the plan. Reggie and I will go ahead and scout out what is causing the smoke. Handmaiden and Foltz will hang back and bring Zoodle."

Brian turned to take a harder look at the terrain we were about to go through and over. He advised, "Also, by the looks of the terrain ahead, you will have to ditch the sled. You won't be able to use the sled on that terrain."

We put the plan into action. Brian and Reggie went ahead to scout the area for us. Handmaiden and I ditched the sled. With what strength we had left, she and I picked Zoodle up. We slung his arms around our necks and proceeded to concentrate on making our way forward.

Handmaiden and I stumbled along, dragging Zoodle's dead weight. Zoodle was completely unconscious. He was breathing only because of his autonomic nervous system.

I figured the best thing to do was to get our brains working on something else, so I asked Handmaiden, "So, where were you before all hell broke loose?"

She looked at me incredulously for a brief moment, and then realized what I was attempting. With only the briefest of smiles and look of acknowledgement in her eyes, she answered, "I'm an army brat. My parents were in the army. My mother passed away when I was seven. My father and grand-mother raised me. As soon as I was old enough to enlist in the army, I did. I have served in the Marines, the Special Forces, and the National Guard.

"I am now in Delta Force. My father is now the defense minister. He sends me to do missions behind enemy lines. My dad actually recommended me to the head of Asian opera-tions. He is actually the reason for me being here. He is also the reason I am now struggling to stay alive and on the brink of losing my sanity."

I sensed that Handmaiden was definitely angry and frustrated.

Personally, I would rather be just about *any*where else. Even Alaska or Turkey would be a pleasant reprieve! I would rather be fighting in either country on the front lines with my friends. My fighting friends were my second family. My second family were my brothers in arms.

Instead, I was running around the globe, doing everything I could to stay alive and evade capture. I felt like a bottle of rum being tossed around between college roommates. The college roommates represented every person who had controlled my life for the last ten years, since I was conscripted.

I could not imagine what Handmaiden was thinking during these arduous times. I could not tell if her anger and frustration were pushing her too hard and too far, or if she was mentally strong enough to push back.

What I did know was that this Handmaiden was a differ-ent Handmaiden than the one who left Mumbai with us. This Handmaiden had been permanently affected by her current life circumstances; they had forged her from a different cast.

⌐ CHAPTER 26 ¬
Recovery

ANDMAIDEN AND I WERE dragging Zoodle through the mountains with the little strength we had left. At one point, Handmaiden stumbled to the ground and lost her grip on Zoodle. I could not hold him on my own, so I laid him down beside some rocks. The rocks gave him partial shelter. Then I made my way over to Handmaiden. I tried to move her closer to Zoodle, but she resisted. She began to play the martyr card as she muttered, "Go home, Gary. Leave us here. Zoodle is done, and I may as well be."

I was about to do as she wished, but I thought to myself 'what would Handmaiden and Zoodle do if the situation were reversed?' If I were on the brink of death, what would they do with me? I had to assume that they would carry me across the world until either we found help or I was a corpse.

I had to ask myself, 'Does the fact that Handmaiden and Zoodle are completely exhausted dictate that I not try to save them?' There were two hard truths I had to consider. The first truth was that people do die of exhaustion. The second hard truth was that I did not think I was physically capable of dragging one person and carrying another. Would dragging one person and carrying another kill me in the process?

Still another concept to consider was the unknown. I had no way of knowing if I would find help in fifty yards, or if I would never find help. Based on knowing that I would have to live with this decision for the rest of my life, I knew what the correct decision was. I summoned all the strength I had left in me and did the impossible. I carried Zoodle and dragged Handmaiden beside me.

We dropped all gear we deemed as nonessential. All we had left were our clothes, weapons, and some ammunition. I put Zoodle on my back and Handmaiden leaned on me.

My body screamed bloody murder at me, but I was focussed on the job at hand. My leg felt like it was going to shatter with each step I took. My feet felt like they were being crushed. My knees threatened to buckle. I did not know I could endure such pain.

We wandered for hours trying to catch up to the others or find some shelter. The smoke trail we had seen earlier had completely disappeared. We were lost.

With absolute determination, I kept going. Zoodle, still on my back, had not moved or made a sound. Handmaiden, still exhausted, continued to lean on my right side. She was barely able to move her feet, let alone walk. I was walking down a hill when I slipped. All three of us tumbled down the hill. We smashed into everything in our path. We hit rocks. We hit trees. We hit parts from a crashed plane. I think Zoodle even hit a goat.

When we reached the bottom, I could not move. My body was numb from the trauma of tumbling down the hill. I was powerless to defend us. I was slipping in and out of consciousness. Just before I passed out, I saw a little boy running toward us, away from the flock of goats he was guarding.

When I regained consciousness, Zoodle and I were on a stranger's bed. Handmaiden was on the floor. I sat up and saw a boy watching us sleep. I couldn't be sure who he was because my vision was blurred. The boy resembled the boy who had run to us at the bottom of the hill. When he realized I was awake, he scampered away in a panic.

I didn't know if we were in the company of sympathizers or EPC loyalists. Either way, I knew that we would be dead if it wasn't for the goat boy."

Brooks chuckled and held back a full-blown laugh. After calming himself down, he asked, "What do you mean, 'the goat boy?'"

I replied, "Well, I never knew his name. He did not speak English. 'The goat boy' was just an easy identifier."

"Fair enough. Go on," said Brooks with a pinch of sarcasm.

"I immediately attempted to get off the bed and go after the boy. When I tried to get up, I fell flat on my face. I tried to get up off the floor but I realized I was too weak to get up on my own. I decided that I had no choice but to lie on the floor of a stranger's house in Kazakhstan.

I did not have to lie on the floor very long. A couple men came in and helped me get back on the bed. From the bed, I heard a familiar voice. It was Brian's! With a small smirk on his face, Brian asked me, "Hey Gary, how goes the battle?"

I replied sarcastically, "Well, I can't walk, and my spine feels like it's being pulled out of my back. Other than that, I feel great!"

While Brian was pleased to see us, he let his smirk disappear. He wanted to get to the point. "Well, we don't have state-of-the-art medicine here. The locals have agreed to help us. When we are all able to travel, we will be on our way." Brian turned his shoulder and began to leave the room.

I had questions, and I saw my opportunity to ask them leaving the room with Brian. Almost panicked, I called after Brian, asking him, "How long do you think we will be here? Why do I have my stomach wrapped in what seems to be loincloth?"

Brian stopped dead in his tracks, turned back around, and answered, "I don't know how long we will be here. We might be here for three days. We might be here for three months. In the states you three are in, just be grateful that the boy found you when he did! Also, there was a stick in your abdomen. We don't have any painkillers, so we decided to take the stick out when you were unconscious." Brian walked out without another word and before I could ask anything else.

The next few days were full of random excruciating pains in my abdomen. Sleep was elusive. My legs had lost their walking memory, so I had to learn how to walk again. Brian called my condition 'temporary paralysis.' I vehemently disagreed. While I did not have a technical term for my condition, I called his diagnosis 'malarkey.' I would later find out that Brian was correct.

After learning to walk again, the local 'doctor' had to open my stomach back up to get the splinters that they missed the first time. If I thought my stomach had been on fire when they took the stick out, I now thought they had poured lava in my stomach! It took a while to recover from having the splinters removed, but eventually the pain and fever began to subside.

My next goal was to get back into travelling shape, which took less time than Brian or Handmaiden guessed. I was simply ready to get back on the road home. We were ready to hit the road again. But first our hosts gave us a few going-away presents.

The village Elder began to speak to us in front of the whole village. "It has been a great honour for me, for *us*, to host these freedom fighters in our village. Knowing you are fighting for what is right, we have made you healthy when you came to us sick. You were weak, and we have made you strong. And when you had nothing to give us in return, we still cared for you. So we have a few things to give to you to help you on your journey."

We were all shocked that they even took us in in the first place. And then, in addition to taking us in, they nursed us back to health, and now they wanted to give us their possessions for nothing. That really blindsided us.

The Elder, speaking in his native language, called up some young men who were holding hunting rifles and AK-47s. After them, a group of beautiful young women approached us and handed us each a satchel with food inside. Then children came up to us and handed each of us our vests, which had been restocked with magazines full of ammo.

The Elder turned to us and said, "I wish all of you the best of luck on your journey." He then approached Brian with a map and a compass and said, "The map will guide you to Moscow, and the compass will guide you home. Safe travels, my friends. You will always be welcomed in my village."

Right after the 'ceremony,' we left the village using the map and compass. The weather was particularly harsh. Little did we know that we were in the coldest winter since 1940! We followed the map and used the compass the Elder had provided. Both tools did what he said they would do. The map led us to Moscow.

We were at the headquarters of the EPC. Getting in would be difficult. Getting back out of the EPC headquarters would make getting in look like a cakewalk!

⌐ CHAPTER 27 ⌐
Colder Than Death

W E HAD KIND OF lost track of exactly what the date was. Our best guess was merely a timeframe from mid-April to early September. Lucky us! We found ourselves in one of the most remote cities on earth in the coldest time of the year.

We were having a hard time dealing with how cold it was. Each day was between -50 and -60 degrees Celsius. I had never, personally, experienced such frigid temperatures. It seemed like anything mechanical was malfunctioning because of the cold. We felt kind of like sitting ducks because our guns were frozen!

We'd had no idea that Moscow could be so cold for so long! We had always known, geographically, where Moscow was, but that knowledge had not prepared us for being there! We finally had to admit that our clothing was simply not designed for this weather.

We did not have any rubles, so we knew we would have to barter for winter clothing. After talking with several store managers, we finally made a deal with the manager of a clothing store. The deal got us all outfitted with winter coats and gloves. The deal cost us one of our guns and half of our ammo. Fortunately, the coats and gloves were very much worth the cost.

We now had to focus on getting through the city undetected by the local police and army, which was difficult because they were always on patrol. We also had to find discreet, secure shelter. We needed to be able to sleep in relative comfort, knowing we would not get caught.

We looked all over the area. We looked in abandoned buildings. We even looked in storm vents. All of them were either too exposed to the weather or not discreet enough.

We wandered around like this for a few days. We slept where we could and ate whatever we could find. By the end of our journey through Moscow, all we had were the clothes on our backs, a handgun, and five bullets.

We were trying to sleep in an abandoned car that Reggie was attempting to hotwire. The car would not start, which got Reggie mad. He slammed the wheel with his fist and screamed at the car, "Start, you piece of garbage!" Calling the car 'garbage' was actually quite appropriate.

Zoodle was sitting beside Reggie. Reggie's outburst took him by surprise. He worried that Reggie's outburst might attract unwanted attention. Zoodle turned to Reggie to calm him down, saying in a lower voice, "Reggie, calm down. We'll just try another car. Hopefully one that'll start."

Reggie wasn't buying Zoodle's attempts at calming him down. Reggie snapped back at Zoodle, "Yeah? Well, we've been on the run since Mumbai, and I am sick of it! I am sick of looking over my shoulder. I am sick of worrying about drawing attention. And I'm tired of trying to sleep with one eye open! I am sick and tired of all of it. I've had it! You guys can go on without me. I am done with this!" Reggie grabbed the handgun from the dashboard and put the barrel in his mouth. Before Zoodle had time to react to what Reggie was doing, Reggie pulled the trigger. The gun's hammer made contact with the bullet base and made an ear-piercing bang. The back of Reggie's head exploded. His blood and brains splattered all over us, across the back seat and the back windshield.

We sat there, shocked. Reggie seemed like the mentally strongest of all of us. Obviously, he had been fighting a war in his mind that none of us knew anything about. Reggie had never complained about the conditions we had to go through. There were only moments before his suicide when had he snapped at Zoodle. None of us had any idea that he was quickly losing his private war.

After we got all the blood and brains off us, Brian grabbed Reggie's tags and left. None of us knew how to hotwire a vehicle, so we just had to tough it out for the rest of the winter. We had to tough it out because walking in that cold would have killed us. As it was, the elements were merciless.

So there, in the city slums, we ate what food we could find. We slept where it was dry. We survived like this until early March, when the cold became warm, and the wet dried. We encountered a small band of refugees travelling on foot. They were going to Ukraine. We joined them. Very shortly after joining with the refugees, we left them and headed to Norway. On our way there, we had some excitement.

We were trying to stay off the roads to avoid contact with the EPC. Each night, we built a small fire but beat the burning wood down to embers. We then coaxed heat from the embers. The embers would be harder to see from the roads.

Most nights we were very cold. To conserve what warmth we could, we huddled together. Sleep was a luxury. When I did fall asleep, I would be jostled awake every hour. Most of the time, that hour seemed like a few minutes! I was jostled awake to either move or keep watch. We each took turns keeping watch.

During the day, we would walk for a few hours, rest for a bit, and then repeat. We kept up this schedule for a few weeks.

After those few weeks, it felt like we were back in Kazakhstan where we had started. Happily, we weren't dragging a comatose man! In fact, Zoodle had made a remarkable recovery! Unfortunately, we had no ammo, and the EPC were constantly closing in on us. We would have gotten to Norway in half the time if the EPC had not been hunting us.

We had managed to foil every opportunity the EPC had to catch us. We were doing our best just to 'blend in.' Unfortunately for us, it was kind of hard for a bunch of people walking along the side of the road to just 'blend in.' One look at our group and anyone could guess that we were military!

We came to an intersection. We stopped to check for anything that looked suspicious. Handmaiden, at the lead of the group, looked left, then right, and waved us forward. I crossed the road. Then Brian crossed. When Handmaiden and Zoodle began to cross, a patrol started driving up the road. We had *no* idea where they came from! Handmaiden made a split second decision to signal us to get down in the ditch.

So, there we were, in the ditch, covered with mud. I only remember that it smelled somewhat like Princeton. While the smell somewhat alarmed me, it also reminded me that I was close to home.

We were lying down in the ditch. The convoy was driving by. My heart was racing, and I was sweating like a horse. I had to calm myself down. I was certain that the soldiers would hear my heart beating furiously. I focussed on breathing slowly. Breathing slowly when your adrenaline is pumping is difficult! These moments could be my last, and there was nothing I could do about it! I concentrated on the fact that there was nothing I could do to help my body to relax. Somehow, my body responded by calming down.

As the convoy passed, it was quite clear that while we had seen them, they had not seen us. BONUS! We were able to move, or so we thought.

Brian tapped me on the shoulder and said, "Hey Gary, we can move now."

We both stood up and watched Handmaiden and Zoodle start to cross the road. Handmaiden crosses the road and Zoodle followed. Before Zoodle got across the road, we heard another car coming from where the convoy had come. Zoodle froze. He looked at us and mouthed to Brian and Handmaiden, 'Get him home.' He then bolted off into the woods in the direction we came from. The EPC soldiers went after him, completely ignoring us. I never saw him again.

I wouldn't have made it home without Zoodle sacrificing himself. If he had run toward us, we would all have ended up in Mongolia. Our lives would have been starvation, slave labour, and being tossed around the globe like pack mules. Without Zoodle, I would have ended back at square one. With a heavy, and thankful, heart, I silently said "Thank you, Zoodle."

⌐ CHAPTER 28 ¬

The Secrets Behind
the Handmaiden

WE WERE ALMOST LOST without Zoodle. Fortunately for us, he was not our only guide resource. We had another guiding resource in Brian, who knew this part of the world. He was able to guide us all the way from northern Russia to Norway.

We encountered numerous trucks full of dead bodies, and even more trucks full of injured soldiers. Fortunately, there was very little resistance to us, which told us that we were getting close to the front lines.

We could hear the battle raging just miles away. We couldn't find a good place to rest because there were mass graves of RUD and EPC soldiers *every*where. For miles, the stench of rotting corpses overpowered the clean, fresh, scent of nature.

People always focus on the human cost of war. The reason for focussing on the human cost may be because the war scars on nature are usually temporary.

I stress 'usually temporary' because if the scars are caused by pollution, nature cannot immediately reverse pollution. Pollution is usually a man-made synthetic. A man-made synthetic is contrary to nature. Nature will attempt to change the chemical structure of the pollutant. Sometimes, if given enough time, and the right conditions, nature can change the synthetic's chemical structure until it can be absorbed into nature. But people are playing Russian roulette when assuming that nature can handle a pollutant.

As concerning as non-pollutant war scars are on nature, those scars are temporary because nature is almost supernatural in its ability to absorb scars inflicted by humans. After nature has absorbed the war scars, nature replaces those scars with boundless natural beauty.

When we were passing through acres of what used to be forest, we observed the land. The land had been turned into a lifeless field of dead trees and immobilized machinery. That is where the front had been just a few days ago. Clearly, the EPC had pushed the RUD forces back to a stronger defensive position. I just hoped the EPC hadn't broken into Germany. If the EPC had invaded Germany, my home, as I knew it, would no longer exist.

We followed the EPC offensive all the way to Norway. We were just outside of Kristiansand. From Kristiansand, our plan was to sail home. Brian had gone to get more wood for our fire. I thought this would be a perfect opportunity for me to get to know her a little better.

With a softer voice, just above a whisper, I looked at Handmaiden and said, "Hey, tell me about yourself. You've already told me you're an army brat and that you have been in the military since you could enlist. But tell me more. Tell me some of your accomplishments. Tell me about some of the challenges you've had to overcome." With slight levity in my voice, I added, "And I promise not to tell anyone your secrets you feel compelled to tell me!"

Handmaiden looked at me, initially, with a stern face. Her eyes were suspicious at first. You could almost hear her mentally evaluating any reasons she may have had to be suspicious. Her face softened, and a small grin appeared. She replied, "Well, after all of the time we have had together, I should tell you at least a little about myself." Then, with a smirk, she continued, "You never know, you might have to do my eulogy someday."

"I was born on September 18, 2023. Since I entered the armed forces, I have always felt at home. Her facial expression completely changed as if something had just occurred to her. She quietly exclaimed, "Wait! You don't even know my real name, do you?"

So, perhaps Zoodle wasn't hallucinating after all when he referred to Handmaiden as 'Emma'! This could be interesting! I replied, "No, I don't. All I remember is Zoodle calling you 'Emma' back in Kazakhstan."

Without missing a beat, Handmaiden replied candidly, "Zoodle was calling me by my first name, Emma. My full name is Emma Garner. I am in my forties."

I unintentionally blurted out a laugh. There was just no way for me to believe she was in her forties. I playfully called her on it and replied, "What! Forty? No way you are forty! The way you handle yourself! Your physical presence! I thought you were a young thirty. I have *nev*er thought of you as even a thirty year old! Upper twenties, perhaps, but thirties, no way! And now you say 'forties'? I still don't believe it! How do you do it? You have very successfully, unintentionally, completely impressed me. WOW!"

Handmaiden giggled like a schoolgirl at my reaction. She said, "Well, remember when we met? I was about thirty years old, and you were almost thirty. The years do have a way of ticking by."

I playfully, but immediately, corrected her. "I was twenty-seven years old, thank you very much!" I feigned being insulted over the two years but the smirk on my face told her all she needed to know. I continued, "Just remember, I was not yet thirty when we met."

Brian got back to the camp. He had some dried-out branches in one hand and a flashlight in the other. He must have heard that Handmaiden and I were talking because he butted into the conversation immediately, asking, "What are you two youngsters talking about?"

I replied politely, saying, "We are talking about who we really are. Emma was telling me about herself, and I think you should join in and do likewise."

Brian grinned and said, "Okay, I am in. I am just not going to tell you my age. That's a secret!"

I replied, "Alright. I'm fine with that. Well, Brian, come clean. We are ready to hear about you whenever you are ready to talk."

Brian smiled and said, "Well, first of all, my name *is* Brian. I am a demolitions expert and a field chaplain. I have been in the army since I was eighteen. I intend to keep serving until I am disabled from injury or too old."

We exchanged stories, jokes, and opinions on the war for hours. We shared lots of laughs and some good-natured teasing. I will always remember the last thing Brian told us: "The world has always been at war. Somewhere on the planet, there have always been people on opposing sides of an ideology. But you've *got* to see past the death. You've got to see past the plagues, and past the violence. But once you see past all of the ugly, you see life. You see the life that you must live. You must live that life because not living that life is dying. And dying is not living."

I stood up and began pacing around Brooks's office. I wanted to show Brooks that I had taken Brian's advice to heart. I addressed Brooks, saying, "Since I got back home, I have been trying to 'seize the day.' I have been trying to live what's left of my life to the fullest. You know, I have been in some of the most disgusting and violent places on earth. I have lived those experiences, and now I live with them. Every day, those horrors tap me on my shoulder to remind me that they aren't going anywhere. No matter how hard I try to suppress them. No matter how hard I try to ignore them, they are always waiting to take me over and make me hurt. Sometimes, those horrors just hurt me mentally. Other times, those horrors hurt me by driving me to hurt those I love. That knowledge is why I come to you. I know I have pent up anxieties that I do NOT want to talk about. Fortunately, it is your job to get me to talk about them and come to peace with them. I think they call the process 'debriefing.'"

I sat back down in realization that the war had affected me in more ways than I thought it did. I had always known that the war had affected me in ways that I could not identify. Despite that, I had convinced myself that most of those feelings and anxieties had been dealt with weeks ago. Each time I came to see him, I realized how very wrong I had been. The majority were yet to be identified, let alone dealt with. The majority were still knocking on my front door.

Brooks approached me and began to comfort me. "Hey Gary, don't beat yourself up about what happened to you. What happened to you is precisely that. Your experiences happened *to* you. You did not cause your experiences to happen to anyone else. You did not even cause what happened to yourself! Those experiences were out of your control. The best thing you can do is to simply accept that you are not responsible for what you suffered. Only then can you move on. But first you have to tell me what did happen, at your own pace, of course."

I looked at Brooks with a sigh of relief. I gave him a thank-you bear hug, and followed up with a verbal thank you. "Thanks, Brooks, that means a lot to me. On to Kristiansand."

Kristiansand was similar to Mumbai. The only real difference was geographically. In Kristiansand, the defenders were being pushed out to sea. In Mumbai, the defenders were being pushed into the mainland.

The EPC navy was overpowering the RUD blockade. The clock was ticking. We had to get to the docks. We took every shortcut possible. We evaded every enemy we saw coming our way. Thanks to Brian's tactics, we made it to the docks. Just as we got there, the EPC were obliterating the RUD blockade. There were Valkyries destroying boats even before the boats set sail. Minotaurs were pushing us out into the water. The RUD forces had been decimated. All that was left of the RUD defenses was a few tanks and some fighter jets above. Soon the EPC would demolish the tanks, running them over like they were an afterthought. The RUD fighter jets were seemingly effortlessly shot down with ground to air missiles.

Brian was ahead of us. He was holding onto a small sailboat so Handmaiden and I wouldn't be left behind. I was running as fast as my legs could carry me. I could hear bullets whizzing past my head. Burning jets were falling from the sky, exploding as they smashed into the ground, shaking it. Behind us there was only death. Minotaurs and Draugrs were closing in on us. I could hear their gears screaming and their steel feet hitting the ground with every step.

Then I heard a scream. I looked back. Handmaiden was fighting for her life. She was fighting for her life with a butter knife and a handgun. I later found out that the handgun had only two bullets. As she fought off the soldiers swarming her, Brian was yelling at me to leave her behind. One part of me said to run, the other said to fight. And then I did something I will never regret.

┌ CHAPTER 29 ┐
The Backhand of Life

TOOK MY FIRST STEP towards running into the fray with a dull hatchet. I ran towards Handmaiden. I was willing to die fighting at her side. I was ready to fight until either I was dead or all her attackers were. Then something hit me from behind. I collapsed like a sack of potatoes. For a few minutes, I drifted in and out of consciousness. All I can remember is being dragged away from Handmaiden. She was giving her fight everything she had. Amazingly, it looked like she was actually holding her own fighting off the EPC forces. Handmaiden was the only person I had ever seen who was a lethal opponent using only a butter knife and an empty handgun! It seemed for a few seconds they couldn't touch her. Then she stabbed a soldier with the butter knife. With her knife buried in the soldier, Handmaiden turned around to use her whole body weight to retrieve her knife. At that very moment, a Minotaur viciously backhanded Handmaiden off the dock.

I looked closely at the cockpit of the Minotaur. I saw a young child about 14 years old, who had a wild, evil look in his eyes. His eyes seemed to scream out for revenge. Fortunately for me, luck was on my side that day.

Just as Minotaur pilot aimed his weapon at us, a jet dove nose first into his Minotaur. The ensuing explosion was monumental! I shielded my eyes from the blast. After the initial blast died down, I took a quick look at the wreckage. Everything was black. If a person did not know what a Minotaur looked like, there would be no way of knowing what you were looking at in the wreckage; it was just one big pile of scrap metal.

There were fires burning. Some were burning fuel, and others were electrical fires. There were also burnt and burning body parts. A sudden panic hit me. Where was Handmaiden? Logic dictated that she had not survived the jet and Minotaur collision. With every fibre of my being, I did not want to accept that.

I probably blacked out from the horrific realization that Handmaiden had probably just died. I say 'probably' because the next thing I remembered was being on the boat. My body was very actively being thrown around on the boat because Brian was dodging the EPC fleet as best he could.

Eventually, thanks to Brian's expertise at the helm, we did escape the carnage. We had escaped with hundreds of other soldiers and civilians. When we realized that we were in safe waters, no pun intended, there was a very noticeable, collective, sigh of relief. The atmosphere gradually changed from absolute fear to the very beginning of relaxation. We knew we were escaping to Great Britain and other RUD territories.

The ride to safety on the water was a nice change. It was the first time I had been able to relax since being in the hospital after Princeton, ten years ago. I lay back and rested. We all waited for our boats to dock on the shores of Great Britain.

Brooks was so into the story that he blurted out, "What about Handmaiden? Did she survive?"

I hesitated. I knew the look on my face changed from relaxed to one of mourning. I replied, "No. She's dead. The jet crashing into the Minotaur set the dock on fire. There was no way she could have survived."

Brooks looked down at his notebook then queried, "Tell me how you felt being safe. After all, you had been a prisoner, and you had been on the run for so long."

I crossed my legs and smiled. "It was one of the most invigorating experiences I have ever had. The locals welcomed us. Their welcome felt genuine, as though they were truly glad to see us. Most of them were elderly, but that did not stop them from caring for us until the army picked us up."

"The locals carried us to their homes in, or on, whatever means they had. I was lucky enough to be in the back of a pickup truck. Others of us were put on horseback. One family, the Mackintosh family, cared for Brian, myself, and about six other men. In the Mackintosh family there were four women of varying ages. The eldest was Violet, the grandmother.

"I was sitting in what seemed to be the grandfather's chair when Violet approached me with a bucket of water and a wet rag. She asked, 'I think you have been through a lot, haven't you, young man?'

"I chuckled and replied, 'Well, ma'am, I don't know what your definition of 'being through a lot' is, but I know what mine is. I would have to agree with you. I have been through a lot.'

"As Violet began washing the blood off my face, I asked her, 'Where were you before the world turned into one big warzone?'

"Violet's face turned troubled. After a very brief hesitation, she answered, 'Well, I was with my extended family of eighteen. My husband and myself were the eldest. My husband's two brothers and their wives were the other couples. We had twelve children between us.

'We were happy. We were all working in the family bakery. The men did the heavy lifting and delivered to families throughout town. The women did the baking and selling in the shop. We did this for about ten years. We were about to go on vacation together to Turkey when the Kocatepe Mosque was bombed. So, instead of going on vacation, we went back to work at the bakery. Then, in just a matter of days, North Korea attacked and occupied South Korea.

'We soon found out that the bombs that North Korea had dropped on South Korea came from the newly formed Eastern Powers of Communism. Europe responded by forming a defensive front to the East.'

"Violet paused as if to gain strength to finish her story, and then continued, "When the defensive front was formed, the men left to fight. The men left thirty years ago. I am still waiting for my husband to return.'

"I did not know what to tell her. I did not know if she was a widow or not. But guessing her age, if her husband was still alive, he would have come home. So I comforted her as best as I could. I needed to pass the time until the army came and picked us up, so I told her about my journey.

"Brian and I stayed in the army's custody for a few days for our injuries to finish healing. We had been commissioned to go back to the front lines when we were fit to travel. As luck would have it, when both of us were ready to be deployed, Canada pulled out of the war. I was given a ride home. Brian was forced to stay.

"He walked me to the transport trucks. We were having a happy last few moments together. 'You know, Brian, I feel as though you and the rest of the American forces are being forced to march to your grave.'

"Brian put his arm around me and said, 'Kid, if there is one thing I don't want you to worry about, I don't want you to worry about how I will end up.' Then his face clouded over and he looked me square in the eyes. 'While you still have the chance, live your life to the fullest. If you can, avoid coming back here. Avoid coming back here at all costs. Do not come back here!'

"I nodded in compliance. I began to climb up into the transport truck. Brian said his last words to me: 'I mean it! Don't waste this chance you have, Gary Foltz, to live your life to the fullest. It's a once-in-a-lifetime opportunity that thousands long for but never get. Cherish the opportunity. Ignore the opportunity and you will get viciously slapped by the backhand of life.'

"He watched me as the truck drove off. I watched him until I could no longer see him. I do not know if he survived. If he has survived, I pray for his ticket home when the world regains its sanity."

⌐ CHAPTER 30 ¬
Denouement

"I GOT HOME THE NEXT day. My father was waiting for me at the airport. A week later, I got a letter from Brian. The envelope that the letter came in had Handmaiden's tags in the envelope. The letter said, 'Take care of these. Brian.' I put them with my tags in my room at home."

Brooks nodded in amazement and covered his mouth in concentration. "So that concludes your story?"

I replied, "Yeah. I think I have covered everything."

Brooks closed his notebook, stood up, and proceeded to shake my hand, saying, "Well, Gary, it has been a pleasure working with you. But we aren't done yet. You still have some emotional issues that I want to help you work through, but not today. You have a date to keep. You are having lunch with Miss Wilson."

My eyes widened in surprise. I was actually rather annoyed at this news and objected, saying, "Are you sure I have to go? I did apologize."

Brooks chuckled and proposed a deal to me. "If you go to this lunch, you don't have to see me for a month. How does that sound?"

I rolled my eyes and said, "Well, I guess having lunch with her wouldn't hurt. Maybe it will be nice to meet with her in a relaxed atmosphere." There was actually something therapeutic about saying 'relaxed atmosphere.' With a very small but relaxed smile, I continued, "Well, Miss Wilson, here I come!"

Brooks smiled and handed me his keys. "I want you looking mildly presentable, so here are my car keys. There are fresh clean clothes in my top right desk drawer. Get changed and go have lunch. I want the car and the clothes back here, clean and undamaged, in two hours."

I powerwalked to the clothes and then to the car. I drove to the restaurant to meet with Miss Wilson, the woman I had thrown over my shoulder a few weeks ago. On my way to the restaurant, I was trying to come up with a good way to reinforce my earlier apology. All I could come up with was, 'Sorry I threw you over my shoulder. I won't throw you over my shoulder again.' Although those words sounded quite lame, I was at my wits' end for something better, so I decided to go with them.

Miss Wilson and I were sitting in the restaurant at a small table across from each other. I started the conversation with my rehearsed apology reinforcement. "Kendall, I want to say again that I am sorry I threw you over my shoulder. Throwing you over my shoulder was NO reflection on you. Just a reflex hammered into me by my army training. I did it without thinking. It won't happen again, that's a promise."

Kendall chuckled and looked me square in the eyes. "Don't worry about it. Where I grew up, kids brought chains to school for self-defense. You throwing me over your shoulder felt like old times. You are forgiven."

I sighed with relief and relaxed, saying, "Good. I thought you were going to sue me for assault."

Kendall smirked and replied, "Who are you trying to kid? Right now, I would rather conscript you. You demonstrated some very useful skills!"

I chuckled. This woman was funny. I have always enjoyed dry humour, and Kendall had that dry sense of humour! I did not expect it. We would see where this went. So, I replied, "I understand that you are a journalist doing a study on Canadian war vets?"

Kendall tilted her head, smiled, and replied, "Yes. Yes, I am a journalist doing a study on Canadian war vets."

I leaned back in my chair, crossed my arms, and said, "Well, have I got a story for you…"

EPILOGUE

OVER TIME, AND SEVERAL coffees and lunches, Gary Foltz ended up telling Miss Kendall Wilson his whole story about his time serving in the armed forces. A week after he was done, Kendall published an article about Canadian war vets and their time overseas.

Gary and Kendall then celebrated with another lunch together. They both realized they had truly connected. After the many hours spent together, Gary decided to propose. Kendall was beaming when she accepted his proposal. They eloped a week later.

They now live with Gary's father, and their two children, named Emma and Andrew. Emma is named after Handmaiden. Andrew is named after Dale Andrews, Gary's commanding officer when Gary fought in Canada. Why Andrew and not Dale? Kendall did not like the name Dale, but she loved the name Andrew.

Brian served on the European front lines for five more years. At the end of those five years, he was honourably discharged because of his age. He now lives with his family back home. Brian and Gary still stay in touch.

Brooks ended his career as a therapist after Gary's last appointment. He is now a custodian at a local health clinic.

Brooks loves the job. He no longer has to figure out how to help people. He just cleans and loves it. It helps him cope with his previous career, before he was a therapist.

Gary's old teammates are still alive. They remain in the Mongolian prison, waiting to be released.

The war ended in the year 2074. The war lasted forty-four years. The Kocatepe Mosque bombings started it all. The last death tally was 1.15 billion. There were also many more missing and injured.

AUTHOR'S NOTE

A T THE END OF my first book comes a first author's note. Google said it's a way to connect to the reader; in actuality, this is true because you are holding my words in your hands, reading my first story. But also, this is false, because what if you didn't enjoy my novel or just skipped to the end just to read the ending? But for this book and any other book you must read every bit of it to understand and enjoy the ending.

In this book I have not taken the effects of war lightly, as they should never be taken for granted. Many people can attest to this; the world is still recovering from wars that even occurred over fifty years ago. It may seem that I tried to make this book sound like it's all about explosions and arms blowing off but to me, this book is about mental toughness and perseverance. I try to remind the audience and the world that through thick and thin, we can come back from anything if we have the determination and the ability to work with what we have, no matter the odds.